MORE THAN ONE

Soulmate

Written by
JASMINE CLEMENTE

ISBN: 979-8-9918703-0-6 (eBook)
ISBN: 979-8-9918703-1-3 (Paperback)

Book Design by Hmdpublishing

Disclaimer

This is a fictional memoir of my emotional truth and personal perspective in and around the 2020 pandemic. The names of identifying characters described in this book have been changed to protect their privacy and certain details have been modified. Also, in many cases, I could not remember the exact words said by certain people or exact descriptions of certain things, and so I filled in gaps as best I could. Hence, this book was written by memory, and mine is imperfect. By changing people's names and some basic descriptions, I've done my best to capture the main purpose of the story which is about healing, transformation, and forgiveness without needing to reveal other people's true identity other than my own.

Jasmine Clemente Publishing, LLC

JASMINE CLEMENTE
PUBLISHING

This book is dedicated to all the women who have loved and lost a boyfriend or two – maybe even three or more. Heartbreak after heartbreak, know that every emotion you ever felt was a heartfelt drop from the ocean of universal love. So long as you know that you're always evolving, there will always be love, laughter, and tears. And there will always be you: A Goddess.

Remember, you are your past, your present and your future, which is why your greatest love story will be the journey you take within.

And, to my curly haired free-spirited adventure seeking cousin, (you know who you are), thank you for lighting the spark within me to step out of my own comfort zone. We'll always have our heart-to-heart girl talks in Tulum.

Lastly, to my father, who's been an exemplarily human being teaching me about the power of love. Sometimes, all it takes is one person to make a difference in someone else's world.

"The Greatest Thing You'll Ever Learn, Is Just to Love and Be Loved in Return."
– **Nat King Cole**

Contents

Chapter 1
What Am I Letting Go Of?

There's something mystical about the winds that whisk throughout the Amazon trees as if an ancestral spirit beckoned me from afar. "Let go," it whispered. Intuitively, I felt its divine guidance speaking from thousands of miles away.

But I wasn't quite sure what to let go of? Was it a person? Place? Or the self-identity I had built: a sultry songstress born in the concrete jungle of dreams, New York City.

In downtown Manhattan, cobblestone streets came alive with door-to-door nightclubs, enticing both tourists and socialites into their dimly lit settings and tribalistic beats pulsating through the sound systems. My heart, feeling its energetic pull, would walk toward an entrance as if responding to a soul invitation.

I was always ready to sing one of my records whether on stage or behind a DJ booth as I'd maneuver my way through crowds of people dancing so close, I could smell sweat dripping off their skin. It was euphoric to say the least, uniting with fellow partygoers getting down to the beat of percussionists pounding congas in the room. And whenever it was my turn to perform, I felt just as vibrantly as the rising of a *kundalini-spine-awakening* empowered by the music.

But just as subtly as seconds slip into hours, sometimes we are slow to change even when we know it's inevitable. Should I keep singing or settle down? I questioned when pondering what to let go of. It was a dilemma faced by many women in their thirties, often influenced by societal expectations as we race to beat our biological clocks and meet other cultural pressures.

Even though I knew women who had it all: the career, the husband, and the kids, I felt I had to choose one over the other—as if a man wouldn't want to commit to a female recording Artist. Why not? Where did that idea even come from? Was my lifestyle too eccentric for love?

Sitting on my living room sofa inside of my one-bedroom apartment, I contemplated the definition of "wife material," what she was and wasn't according to society's standards. And what about my own standards—if I even had any? Thinking that I was the one who needed to change if I wanted to "keep" a man.

"Keep a man", the phrase bothered me. I leaned back, pressed my head into the sofa's cushion, and thought deeper.

The only thing I worked on "keeping" was the dignity to live in my higher purpose, which meant more than whether I'd walk down the aisle with someone. Not that I was against true love; I just believed that true love wouldn't be complete if it didn't include self-love.

Eventually, however, there did come a time when I wanted to find someone to connect more intimately with when the noise of the city quieted down. When the nights turned into days and the music faded into silence, who would I sleep beside?

The problem was that I didn't want to sacrifice parts of myself to be "picked" by a man—such an imbalance of power. And yet, as the years passed, I softened my stance and went from being Miss Independent to Miss Vulnerable, losing myself in relationships that took too much from me: my time, my energy, and most importantly, my peace.

I thought maybe my intuitive whispers of "letting go" were divine instruction to rewrite my entire life story. Call me crazy, but even my aspirations of becoming a star began to fade along with my desire for romance. All those nights of pouring my heart out into the microphone turned into man-bashing girl talks over the phone where I caught myself growing bitter. Like stripping naked to refine my soul of its impurities, I started to realize that my inner urge for "letting go" may have been a signal for renewal.

I decided to pack my bags and head to Mexico where I could release my thoughts onto paper during a self-arranged solo writer's retreat. As fate would have it, I discovered that my cousin, Linda, was coincidently traveling in the same direction at the same time. Who knew? Out of all the people in our family, we were the only single ladies setting out to Tulum just a few days apart. Me, at the beginning of the week. Linda, in the middle.

Looking out from my airplane window view, I watched Manhattan's skyline shrink as we ascended above the clouds, relieved to know that in just a few short hours, our plane would land on Mexican soil richly rooted in Shamanism – Something I imagined had a language of its own, spoken beyond words like that of drumming circles in house music. Latin America, the home of ancient Mayan rituals involving plant medicine and cacao ceremonies. What would I find out here that I didn't in NYC? A new perspective? Inspiration? Regrets?

Soul-searching, I was ready for it.

Upon landing at the Cancun International Airport, I skimmed past a group of rifle-carrying, black fatigue militias guarded by K-9 dogs, and felt apprehensive about being stopped.

Something about their presence reminded me of a lesson learned from my ex-boyfriend, Mike, a six-foot-five, ginger-bearded Actor slightly obsessed with watching apocalyptic Netflix shows. I was 36; he was 30, but this "old soul" far surpassed my then-lived wisdom by showing me the depth of human darkness – of course, only after I'd already fallen for him.

Reminded of our doomsday conversations, I felt uncomfortable amidst this military "guerrilla group" and began speed-walking out of the airport, pulling the handle of my four-wheel luggage, which dragged behind me.

"Esperame, por favor!" I signaled to a taxi driver amid an eager crowd.

"Te dondes vas?"

"Tulum!" I answered.

I saw him hesitate, and then jumped into the backseat slamming the door faster than he could change his mind.

He popped open the trunk, tossed my luggage inside and settled into the driver's seat, then handed me a cold-water to quench my thirst as he irritably explained we were about to drive two hours inland toward the Caribbean coast.

I hadn't considered how far Tulum was from the airport, but I was eager to walk barefoot along the sand, letting its grains slide in between my toes like crystals that haven't lost their spark with time.

Time.

Our most valuable commodity was about to be spent staring out the car window, traveling down memory lane amid gravel dirt roads as I reminisced about Mike describing third-world countries in effort to compare them to apocalyptic shows. With such conviction, Mike swore we would live to see the day when modern civilization would collapse – religious institutions, ivory league colleges, governments, Hollywood – all of it. And everything we knew about law and order would crumble in replacement of Marshal Law, but even that wouldn't succeed. Where would we go then? Mike's eyes, big and blue, would grow intense as he warned about the end of days. A bit extreme, I know. But that wasn't how our first conversation began.

Mike had fallen into my life as subtly as a wild card slipping amidst the changing colors of October-Autumn leaves. I never saw him coming, but once he did, I knew change was in the air.

We met at my girlfriend's get-together in her midtown Manhattan apartment, forming an instant attraction the moment we locked eyes. Slightly joking, he compared me to Jennifer Lopez, a compliment I was used to receiving because of my Puerto Rican descent. I still blushed while sipping my glass of wine and then teased over his resemblance to Marvel's God of Thunder, Thor, impressed by his overpowering masculine Viking-type presence and shoulder length ginger hair. He was refreshingly different from other New Yorkers. Despite sharing a bit about the world of film from his hometown in LA, California, it was his nomadic storytelling adventures that attracted me most. He was open to life and that made me open to him.

After the party, we said our goodbyes to our mutual friend and left her building together, seeking some privacy away from the gathering. It was one of those moments when you just knew we were going to become a "thing."

And we did.

Mike grasped my hand beneath city streetlights and guided me through the main avenue exploring trendy-chic-bar lounges, one of them proudly hanging a rainbow flag out front. Upon pushing the door open, the 80's hit song, "Don't You Forget About Me," played amid a carefree crowd of party boys.

Hey, Hey, Hey, Hey

Ooooh, Woah... Don't you forget about me. Don't, Don't, Don't, Don't

Don't you forget about me

Mike didn't show not one single ounce of homophobia. He just boldly walked in as if he owned the place with me by his side, ordering two drinks on the rocks that turned into a toast. "To beautiful strangers," he said, our glasses clicking.

He then leaned in for a kiss. Surprised, I kissed him back despite sweaty men bumping into us. But none of that stopped Mike from turning up the heat when he sucked my bottom lip, softly nibling them despite how his mustache prickled against my mouth – I loved it. His tongue tasted like cranberry vodka in a room filled with cigarette smokers amid 80's music.

I guess Mike felt emboldened to push the envelope a little further because he then slid his hands inside my jeans, reaching for my panties. I instantly jerked back, feeling slightly violated, and yet, something about our steamy connection felt so passionate – I invited him back to my place.

Throwing all precaution to the wind, we dove headfirst into a relationship disregarding our little age gap that completely flew out the window! And since he was new in town, it didn't take long before moving himself in after cooking us a romantic Thanksgiving dinner for two. He was the handsome finger licking Chef, and I was the candlelight table decorator. It was pure bliss as the seasons changed from cool to cold, and from hot to steamy whenever Mike raised my adrenaline underneath the sheets, in the bedroom.

The next few weeks turned into a Hallmark movie when Mike landed a seasonal job selling fresh-cut Christmas trees amid the bustling Union Square outdoor flea market. They smelled of pine, reminiscent of the Forest's clean aroma. Never had I enjoyed the holidays as much as I did whenever I visited him at work, wandering through aisles brimming with lights and festive decorations that glowed against chilly nights.

"Pick a tree! Any tree! There's millions to choose!" He'd offer, arms wide open.

Holding up a hot cup of coffee in hand, I sarcastically admitted, "I choose you. You're tall enough to be a tree."

He smiled, whipping out his cell phone for selfies. I combed my fingers through my tangled hair trying to match my Irish Norwegian boyfriend's good looks who rocked one left earring and ponytail. Thor had nothing on him.

Later that evening, he carried a tree down the subway steps whistling "Jingle Bells." I loved every minute of it, my inner child beaming with joy as we reached the Brooklyn bound platform. With a Christmas tree to bring home, I finally felt like I'd reach some type of normality in life. For that I was grateful.

Before him, I'd either be singing all-nighters inside of a recording booth wearing sweatpants, or I'd be dressed like some hot celebrity attending swanky industry events. The holidays wouldn't change my work ethic; I'd just continue hustling straight through the new year. It wasn't until meeting Mike, that I actually felt a glimpse of the Christmas spirit.

But just as we settled home and positioned our Christmas tree in the perfect corner, I noticed the smell of Vodka escape his lips, only this time, it didn't sit as well with me as it did during our first night at the bar. One by one, I continued hanging sparkling gold and silver ornaments throughout empty branches, wondering if he'd been drinking again. After topping the tree with a gold star, I walked over to my refrigerator, took out his 6-pack case of Ice Tee Lemonade and discovered he'd been hiding alcohol inside each of them. That's when I knew. Mike was an alcoholic.

Never had it crossed my mind that after several weeks of bringing back 6-packs behind the guise of Ice Tee Lemonade, he'd been spilling out the juice. Holding the refrigerator door open with a can in hand, I gave him a troubling look.

He arched his eyebrows before dropping the base in his voice. "I drink, alright!" He yanked the can from me and took a sip. "The world isn't as kind as it looks. Drinking helps me cope."

"Fuck," I whispered. "Another one."

"What did you say?" Mike asked. "Speak louder."

"Another one!" I yelled. "Another man coming to steal my light. So, let me guess? You're an alcoholic!" I slammed the refrigerator door.

"I DRINK! Everyone has baggage!" He defended. "It's called life! And you think you're older than me!? I'm more mature than you!"

"You're not more mature; you just look older because alcohol AGES YOU!"

On and on we argued. Every moment more intense than the last as if some hot air balloon had just popped our two-month honeymoon period. Despite him already being aware of his own drinking problem, I'm sure he believed I wouldn't have discovered it since he'd been concealing alcohol inside of Ice Tee cans for weeks. Eventually however, we cooled down and had a heart-to-heart.

"Jazz..."

"Yea?"

"I was raped as a kid," Mike admitted.

My heart sank. I had no idea.

For the rest of the night, he admitted to being sexually abused inside a trailer park home. Then it all made sense – why he drank to numb the pain. At barely 15 years old, he ran away and headed straight for Hollywood in pursuit of an acting career but ended up couch surfing, never staying in one place long enough to call home. It's also why he didn't just move from couch to couch, but from city to city.

I couldn't fathom what it must've felt like for a young boy to be taken against his will, adjusting his behavior for an abuser that forced himself upon him until he was old enough to escape. No wonder he knew how to slip in and out of character; a survival technique he must've learned growing up.

That night, I witnessed a vulnerability within Mike's blue eyes that broke my heart, and the heroic man who resembled Thor didn't seem so invincible anymore.

It became obvious that the situation was risky. All the red flags, providing a way out before I got too involved. But after all, it was Christmas: symbolic of forgiveness and love. And so, despite knowing there was a strong possibility that Mike would become a "lesson" instead of a "lifetime partner," I also knew his presence was a gift, even if it came wrapped in darkness. In fact, how could I dismiss all the joy he made me feel – those home cooked holiday dinners, nights at the Christmas market, and warm companionship of unstoppable laughter – just because of the sadness that came with it? Weren't both emotions just as real as the other? I couldn't deny the yang part of the yin.

Before going to bed, he grabbed the remote and signed into Netflix, selecting an apocalyptic series. It wasn't romantic, but it was real. As each character went through the depths of despair trying to survive the direst of situations, it soothed him.

"These aren't just television shows, ya know?" He said. "This is really gonna happen one day and you better be prepared when it does."

I thought him to be a little mad, perhaps even psychopathic. But as crazy as it sounds, he might've been right. If so, who better to prepare for an apocalypse than someone who already knew what it was like to really survive on their own – without *any* support?

But his warrior traits came at a price, obviously. From what I started to see, Mike viewed love as a weakness.

We had plans for him to meet my family. This wasn't just a big deal for him, but it was a big deal for me – the long lost relative – to show up on a holiday I normally didn't celebrate.

Wearing a flattering dress in heels, I waited for him to come home so we could leave together but as the clock ticked, hour after hour, no sign of him appeared. Eventually, I slipped my heels off and stared at my Christmas tree hoping he would walk through the door. But not one text came all night. I called my relatives and canceled.

Unable to sleep, I tossed and turned in bed, wondering why he had played such a cruel joke.

The next morning around 7 am, he quietly arrived without mentioning so much as a single word about the night before. Forget about being a 36-year-old woman. I began crying as if I were an abandoned child lost at sea, or worst, a gutted fish bleeding in the middle of the ocean.

Why did I take it so hard? I'm aware that there are different types of women in the world; some who wouldn't have given Mike's "ghosting" a second thought. With her head held high, she would've locked the door behind and strutted her sexy self into the festive evening wearing a sparkling, sequin dress without breaking a sweat. I imagine her opening a pocket-size mirror to paint her lips red saying, "Fuck it." But for me, his disappearing act did a double whammy. First, because I worried about him. Secondly, because I felt rejected on the biggest family-oriented night of the year. Call me naïve, but I was hoping to plant roots together.

Finally, he spoke.

"I rode the train back and forth last night. Slept on it to the Bronx and back."

"No, you didn't," I said.

He slicked back his soft ginger hair. "Are you calling me a liar?"

"There's no word to DESCRIBE what you are," I fumed, tears flowing. I cried until the tears dried my skin, confused and curious about his whereabouts the night before. Mike removed his boots to make himself more comfortable and then grabbed the remote in search of another apocalyptic show. "Come on, it's Christmas, lighten up. We'll watch a movie."

Are you fuck'n kidding me? I thought, was he a narcissist or a psychopath? One was more perilous than the other.

"We're all a little fucked up," I confessed. "I got my issues, too. But that's why I thought this Christmas would be different. Shit, my entire life I wouldn't bother celebrating it because I was so fixated on becoming a Singer... Honestly, I never even wanted a conventional life, whatever the fuck that is anyway."

Mike found a post-apocalyptic show called, "The 100," a series about a group returning to Earth's uninhabitable atmosphere. To think, if such a thing were to really happen, I wonder what society would do differently to rebuild itself?

After pressing play, it reminded me of the time I discovered he was an alcoholic because he avoided tough conversations by getting lost in the dramatics of survivor shows; assuming some of the characters mirrored his hardcore exterior.

I still wanted to know where he'd been the night before, but he never told. Instead, he admitted one thing: he wasn't too keen on meeting my family because he feared they'd judge him. And I couldn't disagree; they probably would.

They weren't exactly the compassionately humanitarian type to take people in and make a difference. In fact, they were your "keeping up with the Joneses" type. Not that there's anything wrong with money and affluence. Heck, I wouldn't have pursued a career in entertainment if I were against living prosperously. *Hello, Hollywood!* Known for fame and fortune. My point is, one whiff of a troubled soul and they'd probably give him the cold shoulder after judging my so-called "bad choices" in men.

But life isn't that black or white. Is it?

Although they never got the chance to meet Mike, I'm sure as soon as they would've noticed he had an alcohol problem, they would've warned me to stay away from him. And maybe... just maybe... Mike experienced this before.

I understood that nobody was flawless; not my family, not myself, not even society. And if it were wrong to judge someone without having walked a mile in their shoes, then it was a lesson we could all benefit from. Or at least... I could.

I couldn't help but notice how Mike's eyes swelled as if he were holding back tears. Actor or not, I believed his pain was genuine. Therefore, wherever he might've disappeared to on Christmas Eve – whether he rode the train back and forth drinking booze all night, or if he were celebrating it with someone else drinking Eggnog – I understood why it was easier for him to escape rather than tell the truth. I brought up AA as an option, to which he rolled his eyes, murmuring how he'd done it all before. Did he?

To my understanding, AA involved a twelve-step program that introduced the idea of God being available whenever you needed to seek guidance through prayer. Unsure of whether Mike ever attended AA, I knew he believed in a higher power because of our deep conversations during apocalyptic shows. And with that, I figured I'd *let go and let God.*

Weeks passed. One day, just as I believed we had moved passed a rather dramatic incident, I returned home from work to find my laptop left wide open on the kitchen table. When I walked over to close it, I noticed an outgoing email. What I saw next, changed everything.

Dick pics! It was an exchange of pictures between Mike's penis and someone else's as if to compare who's is bigger, emailing back and forth about dates and times to hook up. I wanted to rip my hair out of my head from missing the signs. How didn't I know?

As I delved further into the screen, I read details about Mike inviting his lover over to my place during my working hours. I took a screenshot and sent it to Mike. "Don't bother coming back," I text.

But... he had to. With all his belongings left at my place including clothes, shoes, and suitcases, where else would he go? And, so I knew, that after I sent him that text, it meant war.

Not more than an hour later, I looked outside my window and saw Mike pacing back and forth as if he were thinking of what to say. Finally, he charged up the steps and barged right in.

I questioned why he lied about being with a man. Stomping his feet across the room, he exploded in tears. "I'm confused! I don't know if I'm gay or straight! I don't know what I want!"

I felt like the ultimate bitch. What do I do? Should we have another heart-to-heart, or is he faking it? I didn't know what to think. I just knew that when I had asked the universe to bring me a soulmate, I was in no way, shape, or form, prepared to handle how it showed up.

"For Christ's sake, it's only January. We just went through that whole Christmas saga and now we're starting the New Year like this," I complained.

It suddenly dawned on me; how selfish I was being for only thinking about myself when this human being was having a total meltdown. Did I have to be so cold-hearted when I had never been in his shoes? He was raped as a child. Of course, that influenced his psyche.

Finally, Mike collapsed at the edge of my bed and began sobbing with his head in hands. I put on my tough-girl persona and accused him of guilt-tripping me so I wouldn't kick him out. He stopped, looked up at me and said, "Oh, so now I'm not allowed to have feelings?"

Again, I felt like an even bigger bitch.

I didn't know what to believe or if wanting to protect myself from further heartbreak was wrong? But as I watched Mike cry in front of me, something inside of myself wanted to help. *Could* I stop him from crying? *Should* I stop him from crying? What if crying were good for his soul? The more he wept, the more I sensed his inner child crying for the help he never received growing up. And then I realized that Mike must've been with a man on Christmas Eve and that's why he never told me where he was. And perhaps, my apartment was his safe space to call home as if what he needed from me was a mother's love instead of a girlfriend's love because like he said, he didn't know if he was gay or straight – which also meant that I didn't know where I stood either.

For hours we spoke, and four hours we cried. Neither of us knowing what to feel – what was right or wrong? But what we did know was that we each wanted to be heard, understood, and loved. And that was the truth of it all.

As the day weened into night, we eventually worked things out and eased into each other's arms, snuggling in bed as our emotional bond grew stronger. No more masks; this was real. I started to get used to this merry-go-round and admittedly wanted us to stay together. Where there was a will, there was a way. And with enough love, maybe we could heal.

But after a few days, Mike left again. This time, with all his belongings. Was this his norm when it came to couch surfing? Had he done this to every partner before? Just when I had started to get used to having him baked into the fabric of my daily life, he disappeared. I just hoped that wherever he went this time, he'd be okay.

It was then that I realized, as I looked upon the collection of dust particles floating amid the empty space where our Christmas tree once stood, that some things can be here today and gone tomorrow. Just like that. A lost love. A dream.

Although I didn't know how Mike's story would end up, I knew I had to turn the page just like songs that fade after a few minutes of melody, waiting for the next to play. If I had learned anything from Mike, it was this: Whether you decide to run away or decide to stay, you have to keep on moving. That's how you let go of yesterday.

Chapter 2
Beyond The Rain, The Sun Still Shines – Solo

My cab driver stopped at the traffic light. "We're almost there," he announced.

"Finally!" I screeched, looking outside the car window.

Beach therapy is what everyone yearns for when leaving a big metropolitan city. But the further inland we drove, the darker the clouds appeared on the road, obscuring the tropical scenery with a misty fog. I rolled up my window to prevent drizzles from reaching in.

It was barely 2 pm when we finally reached my tribal-themed glamping hotel, still early enough to explore the town.

After checking in my luggage, I excitedly walked to the nearby rooftop café where a tall, handsome, blue-eyed waiter escorted me up its spiral staircase. "Bienvenida," he greeted, leading the way with a menu in hand. Oddly enough, he coincidently resembled Mike, as if the universe was affirming that my memories of him were beautifully intertwined with my current journey. Alas, I settled at an outdoor table and chose to order an exotic flower-infused ice-cold drink, a refreshing way to kick-off my vacation.

However, as I looked out into the distance, I noticed a profusion of dark clouds looming over the coastline, bringing a sudden wickedness that sent waves ferociously crashing into shore. Anxiously, I Googled the weather forecast on my phone. WTF!? Thunderstorms were predicted for the next seven days!

I tried to embrace the moment, not wishing it was anything different except for whatever life was presenting me – good or bad. But even as I admired a flock of birds flying off the rooftop's ledges, my fear intensified.

Time was of the essence. Since I knew my cousin, Linda, wouldn't arrive in Tulum for at least a few more days, I had to think fast. Within seconds, a heavy downpour sent me running back down the stairs and into the water-puddled streets to get as far away from what seemed like a living, breathing Kali-Ma, the black Hindi Goddess of doom.

Once I returned to my glamping tent, I leaped into bed and pulled the blankets over my head like a frightened little girl. Outside my tiki hut, tropical winds gained momentum, causing its thinly made fabric to blow inward, secured only by a flimsy zipper. Hail pelted down, creating a stream of mud to trickle underneath the tent as thunder rumbled ominously, cracking open the sky – a maddening confrontation between man and nature, or woman and witch.

Which one am I? I question after opening my laptop to begin typing about this harrowing experience. Trembling, my fingers quickly skated across the keyboard, trying to capture every detail of what would turn out to be the longest and loneliest night of my life.

Pausing to inhale and exhale deeply, I shifted my perspective and saw the storm as a gift. They say rain washes away the old, releasing what no longer serves us like tears exploding from our eyes. Perhaps then, the Book Gods poured rain to bless my journey as I began writing my story in the middle of the Mayan jungle, a choice I had made to follow my intuitive whispers of *letting go* as if something was nudging me to leave town and clear my head. Who will I write about? How much will I tell? And why specific men and not others? Mike hadn't been the only man to kiss my soul with a tortured twist.

Sometimes, there are just those few who shatter our hearts into a million pieces, leaving us to repair ourselves like a hurricane uprooting our lives from a change of weather or a change of heart. And so, how can we forget those experiences that catalyzed our growth? Like this one, when the frightening bang of thunder sends me running out of my tiki hut towards the lobby.

"I can't take this anymore! Permiso," I yell to the front desk, losing my breath from a fast-pounding heart. "I might need to cut my trip short and return to the airport."

A beautiful Mexican brunette looks up at her manager towering over her at six feet tall. He chimes in. "We understand your concerns. Pero, the weather constantly changes, y manana lo viene el sol."

I think about the 2004 Thailand Tsunami that rushed in without warning and didn't care to take chances. "But what if the storm turns into a crazy hurricane!? That tent will just blow away like some fuck'n Wizard of Oz scene! Lo siento, pero, yo tengo mucho miedo."

They both try hard not to giggle. It was then when I realized how out-of-place I was as a bona fide New York city girl.

"Estas bien," He smirks. "We'll upgrade your room, but I'll need you to return the keys from your safety lockbox."

I blow a sigh of relief. At least now, I wouldn't have to worry about a straw-woven rooftop caving in over my head.

At that moment, when we exchanged keys across the lobby's wooden counter, I noticed that I was trading a number 10 keychain for a number 11, which together sequenced 111. It might sound strange to some, but for me this was a sign of angelic protection.

Entering my new room, I scan the earth-tone gravel cemented walls adorning two symmetric lampshades emanating a warm glow right above the master bed and instantly felt like it was a home away from home. Unlike the tent, this room had a bit more furniture: a cream-colored futon sofa, some wooden tables and a small refrigerator. It wasn't much, but my spirit felt soothed by the Indian deity, Ganesha, a large wooden elephant centerpiece that stood amid a walnut coffee table, representing the remover of all obstacles.

I walk over to the bed and sit on its edge to reopen my luggage, once again pulling out my laptop. This time, I'll travel back into time as I write about the calm *before* the storm in a different environment with a different vibe. But first, I change out of my wet clothes and slip into something comfier.

After sliding into bed, I fluff up two pillows behind my neck and think, "If I could make it through the night in this foreign country alone, then I can write this damn book."

Minutes pass. I lay there caressing my legs amidst cotton blankets without a single word to write, wondering what it would be like if I had a husband to make love to in this bed, his masculine arms sheltering me during a tropical storm.

Instead, I lay safely cocooned inside of my hotel room – single – yet free. To my left, I see rain smearing down the windowpane and can't help but slip into a nostalgic period of when my poetic soulmate, Pierre, entered my life. Not that it was raining on that Winter's Harlem night, but because our enchanting connection seemed to have been orchestrated by something more divine. For now, we'll call it destiny.

Was it the wine, the weed, or the candlelight that made the mood just right? Or was it the way his French-infused Creo-African spirit raised the heat of my tropical Latin blood whenever his chestnut-colored eyes met mine?

"Want more wine?" Pierre asked. I nodded my head. "Sure."

Amidst the amber glow of our surrounding tealights, I noticed his black beaded mala bracelet slide down his wrists as he poured me a glass. It was his protection bracelet; a symbolic jewel he wore every day as a fashion statement – carrying purpose and meaning. After ensuring my comfort with some wine, he lit up his vape pen and took a puff.

"I like all these tealights," I said.

"Yea, it can make any shitty apartment look romantic," he laughed before extending the flame to a few more candles that would spark a creative atmosphere.

His home was far from a fancy loft or upscale Manhattan penthouse. Like most people who run to the city in search of big dreams, it was a small one-bedroom apartment, perfect for a struggling Artist who'd built an at-home recording studio accented by a wall collection of culturally driven historical books. Every title impressed me, offering glimpses into his intellectual world, which in my eyes, made him even more attractive. I especially loved it when he'd stretch my musical palette by introducing me to old songs from the back of his vinyl crates, just like his song of choice for the night, "West Wind," a secret classic by Nina Simone.

The more I drank, the more I slouched back into my seat. He sat across from me, the two of us sitting in front of his Pro

Tools-ready desktop computer, preparing to remake this lost chant with the revival of my vocals.

"What made you choose this song?" I asked.

"It's different," he answered, adjusting his headphones for the session. "Nina's singing over some African drumming, wailing as if some spirit hijacked her body. That's why I like it for you. The only difference is, you're gonna make this record *your own*," he winked.

He was already high off his vape pen, and I was already tipsy off my glass of Moscato when I brought my mouth closer to the mic and softly blew an airy adlib. Under pressure, I paused momentarily, took one last sip of wine, and then closed my eyes.

At first, I saw nothing, only darkness. I wanted it that way. I wanted to feel the music and enter its melodic world by leaving mine behind. When the beat dropped, the drum rhythms began pulling at my heartstrings until every note married my cells, baptizing me into the emergence of my alter ego: A Songstress.

Finally, I sang:

Here, within my heart.

Here, within my soul.

I hear my angels whisper to sing my song.

Despite singing inside of a home recording studio within a four-wall bedroom, this New York reality was no match for the paradise within my mind, especially when the drumming had a power of its own as I continued singing with the spirit of alcohol coursing through my veins until the last hand smacked the last drum.

When I am lost, I close my eyes, and in the dark,

I find,

I find my north star, my north star

Stretching "star" for as long as possible, I felt drunk off the image of a distant star as this mantra traveled through my throat chakra. From the corner of my eyes, I noticed Pierre looking at me with wide eyes of wonder, witnessing the magical trance I had fallen under. Finally, only a few light drum clacks sounded until my voice faded into whisper.

Pierre stopped recording. "This was fuck'n perfect!" His headphones slid off his earlobes, landing around his neck.

There it goes again, that look between us. After accomplishing something we could call our own, a special bond was born in a moment that could never be stolen. But I still wanted to go another round.

"I don't know about keeping this," I confessed, twisting my curly hair into a bun as if the night had just begun.

"No! Are you crazy!? What we captured here is magic! I don't know what the fuck possessed you, but we don't need to touch it!"

I scanned his bedroom, admiring the hall-of-fame Jimmie Hendrix portrait that hung above his King-size mattress with the legendary Bob Marley across from it and sighed. "OK. We'll keep it."

After mixing down the music, he searched for an R&B playlist. I moved away from his desktop and threw myself on the bed, deciding to rest my drunken head on his pillow. Music playing, candles burning, and too much wine causing dizzy spells, Pierre crawled into bed and came in for a kiss, but just as fast as he leaned in, he pulled back.

"What's wrong?" I asked.

He lay on his backside, looking up toward the ceiling. "I'm not sure if we should do this."

"Is it Rebecca?"

"I don't know. I like you a lot. It's just that... This might be wrong." He continued staring into space.

I wasn't drunk enough not to understand what was being said, so I raised myself up and planted my feet on the floor.

He pulled the back of my shirt, "You can't leave in the middle of the night."

"Don't act like you care now!" I pushed his hands off. "You know we have something special. It's undeniable the way we look at each other. But you're gonna doubt what we have over an ex?"

"Nah... it's not like that."

"Then, what's it like?"

He took a deep breath. "I know I told you we've been on and off for a while, but we just went to see *Black Panther* over the weekend."

"So, you went back to Rebecca again! For the hundredth time?" I felt like someone had punched me in the gut.

Pierre squinted his eyes. "You didn't wanna see *Black Panther* anyway! You wanted to see that 50 *Shades of Grey* bullshit!"

"Yea, because I wanted to see something romantic for Valentine's Day. You know... A love story?"

"Fuck that movie! Ain't it about some rich white people doing some sadistic bullshit in the bedroom?"

"I wouldn't know! I haven't seen it yet! But nice to know you went back to Rebecca while I was home crying!"

"I'm not back with her! We just went to the movies."

"You went to the movies with someone who's in love with you! You don't think that's a little misleading?"

Pierre took a deep breath. "That's why I don't think we should do this... I'm confused."

Pushing my disappointment aside, I laid my head back on the pillow and knew deep down how important it was for him to watch *Black Panther*. It was the first African American Marvel comic book film to ever hit the big screen, making it a historical moment. Yet, because I'd been more concerned with watching *50 Shades of Grey* for Valentine's weekend, I didn't realize that by stepping into someone else's world to show them that what they care about, you care about too, is how you create your own real-life romance novelty. I decided to have an honest conversation with him.

"Look, what makes you and I special is that we're friends before lovers."

"True," he smirked. "But even though you're like a sister to me, I'm so fuck'n attracted to you."

"I know. It's kinda sick." We both chuckled, facing each other in what became pillow talk amidst the bedroom's candlelit glow.

"It's like, one minute we're caught in this love triangle, and the next, we're besties. So, talk to me," I said, sinking my head into one of his pillows. "What's really going on with you and Rebecca?"

Pierre pulled out his vape pen and took a few hits of some special kind of CBD oil to relax him before talking. After exhaling, his shoulders dropped like a feather lightly falling. He seemed peaceful, laying back comfortably beside me.

"Every year on the 4th of July, I throw a rooftop party in my building. Last Summer, a bunch of us were watching fireworks, when out of nowhere, Rebecca got down on one knee and proposed."

"She did what!?" I arched my eyebrows. "She gave you a ring?"

Pierre took another hit from his vape. "Nah, nah... No ring, but still, that shit sent me RUNNING!" He emphasized. "She wanted the house, the kids, the whole nine yards, but I wanted to go hard with my career. Do you know what it's like to be in your 30s and see all your friends get cast on Netflix while you ain't got shit to show? All Rebecca ever talked about was getting married and buying a house while I was a broke actor, still living in this one-bedroom apartment... still chasing a dream."

"She sounds like a lot of women," I shrugged my shoulders. "I think the concept of marriage is ingrained so deeply in our heads. It's hard to shake off."

Pierre continued, "I never meant to hurt her, but she knew where my head was at. Anyway, after we broke up, I went dead silent. Then, BOOM!" He smacks his hand on the bed. "I came back from the dead and reached out to her! Do you know how much it would destroy her if I left again? And now, here you come along," he leans in, moving closer as he looks into my face, eyebrows arched. "Maybe it's because we're both Artists, but I just feel like everything's so much easier with you but... I can't hurt her again." He breaks his gaze from me and looks down.

I felt flattered and yet doubted his sincerity. Was he a player? A cheater? A liar? Or was he genuinely confused? He was human – that much I knew. Who's perfect, anyway? Don't we all get confused? I believed he was just trying to figure things out like I was.

"Pierre, was I your rebound?" I asked.

"You wanna talk about rebounds?" He snapped. "What about that white boy, Mike, who popped up at your doorstep when I was first getting to know you?"

I shot back. "I had no idea Mike was coming! He knocked on my window with a bagel and coffee to apologize for the way we broke up. I thought talking face-to-face would be good for closure, so I let him in. When I told Mike I was dating someone new, he left and didn't come back, so you can't even *compare* Mike to Rebecca."

"Bullshit! He lied about being gay by sleeping with a man behind your back! But all it took was A BAGEL AND COFFEE FOR YOU TO FORGIVE HIM?"

"WOW," I said. "Maybe I should leave." I raised myself up from bed and threw the pillow.

"Jazz, wait... I'm sorry. I don't want you to go... I'm just confused."

"Mike was confused, too! He didn't know if he was gay or straight! But the reason I accepted his apology is because he'd been through the kinds of things in life that – THANK GOD – you never did!"

"Oh, so you're defending him now!?" Pierre yelled.

"It's not about defending him! It's about the fact that I have the kind of closure with Mike that you don't have with Rebecca! So, since the timing isn't right, I'll just go," I shook my head.

Pierre grabbed my hand and stopped me from leaving. "Wait. I'm not done talking!"

"Fine," I said. "Just don't judge me since I'm not judging you."

Pierre agreed.

"Look, I don't wanna commit to anyone right now. Honestly, I don't even wanna be with Rebecca, but I can't talk to her the same way I can talk to you. The other thing is that she takes antidepressants because she lost a baby once. So, I'm afraid she won't be able to handle another breakup..."

I released my messy bun and let my hair fall loose around my shoulders. Then, I scratched my head and thought of what to say. Even though I hadn't met Rebecca, there's an unspoken respect between women as feminists. Discovering she had lost a baby is something I'd never wish upon my worst enemy. I decided to choose my words carefully by being gentle about the state of her mental health and yet fair to Pierre's needs as well.

I rolled up my sleeves and made myself a little more comfortable. "That's a lot of guilt you're carrying." I told him. "I wouldn't wanna break someone's heart either, so I understand. But.... And this is a big *but*.... When you left her the first time, you told me you released a burden off your shoulders. The problem is, it'll be harder to leave again. I'm not trying to convince you to be with me because if you don't wanna be with anyone right now, you shouldn't. Wait. Hold that thought," I reached for the bottle of Moscato that stood on his nightstand. "I need more wine for this."

"Hey, you look too tired to leave. Let me give you some sweatpants," Pierre offered. "Stay 'till the morning."

"I appreciate it," I smiled, then gulped down the last of my drink.

After changing, I crawled underneath the sheets. He blew out the candles and lay beside me. The two of us listened to music off his Amazon playlist until our eyelids fell heavy, fading to the current song, "Best Part," By Daniel Cesar and HER.

You don't know, babe
When you hold me
And kiss me slowly
It's the sweetest thing

Pierre spooned me from behind, his hands pressing deeper into my skin as he held my waste. We were drunk tired, or in his case, hazy tired, and too comfortable to continue our conversation. As the energy got the best of us, we fell asleep to the music.

I just wanna see how beautiful you are
You know that I see it
I know you're a star,
Where you go, I'll follow

No matter how far
If life were a movie,
Know you're the best part
Ohh ohhh, You're the best part

The next morning felt like a dream I didn't want to awake from. I could feel Pierre's lips touch my earlobes when yawning from behind, his face gently snuggled next to mine. Eventually, he unlatched himself from our sleeping cocoon. And with all the space to stretch out in his bed, it made waking up even harder. Especially from the way the sun's glare slipped through the windows of his jungle-enthused fire escape, blessing the start of our day with natural sunlight. It was a real NY scene, an array of looping vines wrapped around rustic zigzagging stairs to make up for the lack of nature in this robust city. Indeed, it was a sight I didn't mind waking up to.

Too enamored to part ways, Pierre invited me to accompany him to the Battery Park fishing pier. It was his happy place where the view of the water made him feel most peaceful, even though it was still the middle of Winter.

Rushing to grab the downtown number 1 train, we quickly swiped our metro cards through the turnstiles and ran for the closing doors.

As the train rumbled through the underground tunnel, Pierre kept close to my body, ensuring he didn't lose me in the crowd as I grabbed a pole. Once steady, he handed me one of his earplugs.

"Put this on."

"Only one?" I asked.

"I'll keep one in my ear. You keep the other in yours."

And just like that, we listened to the same songs the whole way there, tuning into the same frequency just like we'd done the night before.

It was during moments like this that made me fall deeper in love because we didn't need any fancy dates or expensive dinners to connect soul to soul. Despite being amongst strangers on a packed train, Pierre was all I needed to feel safe.

But when we exited the station, I started to get a strange feeling inside my gut. I knew that feeling – my intuition trying to tell me something. Nevertheless, he took my hand and led me to the pier until we found a bench to sit and enjoy the view.

A trail of golden sunlight sparkled amidst the water's surface, providing just enough warmth on that thirty-something-degree, mild Winter's Day. Tourists roamed the area, and some couples walked hand in hand watching sailboat's cruise by the Statue of Liberty. It was the picture-perfect postcard scene. Another memory frozen in time that I could never forget.

Pierre pulled the front of my jacket towards him. "Come here," he ordered. I knew consequences could follow because of his "situationship" with Rebecca, but I did as told and brought my lips towards his, knowing there was no amount of Winter blues that could ruin the warmth between us. Still, my intuition grew louder, and for some reason, I pulled back, breaking our little love spell. "Pierre, have you spoken to Rebecca today?"

He let go of my waist. "Why'd you bring up her name? We just spoke about her all fuck'n night."

"I know, but I have this uneasy feeling in my gut that won't go away. I think you should call."

He rolled his eyes. "Yeah, I probably should. Fuck!" Annoyed, he walked off.

Call it female intuition, but despite not wanting to confuse him any further, I felt like I could feel Rebecca from afar and didn't want her left in the dark. Why did I care about her feelings when she was the competing woman? I don't know why, but I did.

From where I stood, I could see Pierre talking on his cell phone. I imagined him trying to break it off but probably couldn't find the right words to say. I knew it must've been difficult, but at least that feeling inside my gut disappeared.

While waiting, I looked out at sea allowing my thoughts to drift with the wind that blew through my hair as every passing sailboat made me think of the missed opportunities we have in life. Once a ship leaves the dock, we have no choice but to wait for the next.

Eventually, Pierre ended his phone call and walked back toward me, chin down.

"It didn't go too well, did it?" I asked.

Pierre grabbed the scarf around my neck and pulled me closer. "I don't wanna talk about it."

I brushed his hands off, "What do you mean, you don't wanna talk about it!? You have to! Did you end it or not?"

"Why can't you just let it go? This decision ain't easy for me."

"Trust me, I get that. But then, we probably shouldn't take romantic walks by the water as if we're more than friends.

In frustration, he pulled down the strings of his hooded sweater, "Jazz, I'm sorry."

"Yea, well, whatever. I should probably go if you're gonna work things out with Rebecca."

"Let me walk you to the train, at least."

"Wow." I shook my head in disbelief. "I don't know why I thought you were gonna come clean. Maybe I gave you too much credit."

I rolled my eyes and continued. "Aside from that, what are you gonna tell her about the song we recorded?"

"Maybe I won't tell her anything."

"Pierre! Whatever you wanna do with your personal life is one thing, but I need to know if you're serious about releasing this record!"

"I need time to think!" he admitted.

I pushed through the NYC crowd, carelessly bumping into people as I walked ahead of Pierre. It seemed incredibly dubious how quickly our connection had turned from hot to cold in just a matter of seconds due to one call by one woman.

Who had more power, I wondered? Her? Me? Pierre? Or fate?

Although I didn't need the Staten Island ferry, we heard its hourly horn go off loud and clear as we headed toward the train station nuzzled next to it. That urgent feeling of "missed opportunities" took over me and I couldn't help but hopelessly look at Pierre like he was making a mistake.

"Wait!" Pierre called out, catching up from behind. "Don't go home. Why don't we go back uptown and work on more music? Or do whatever you wanna do?"

I turned around to face him. "Don't play with my emotions. You're confusing me."

"I'm sorry, Jazz. I don't wanna lose you."

I looked into his eyes, my heart racing as fast as the people running to catch the ferry boat. "I know you're afraid to make the wrong choice, but you're only pressuring yourself. If you break up with her, you can be free to date whoever the fuck you want. That's what being single is all about! Why are you committing to someone you're not even sure of?"

Pierre lowered his hoodie, "I think I'm in love with the both of you."

I looked away from his eyes and scanned my environment as the last few runners sped up to catch the ferry with all their might. Time was of the essence.

"I really... really... wanna fight for you."

The ferry honked its last horn, signaling it had finally left the dock. I looked back at Pierre. "But... fighting for someone and forcing them to stay are two different things."

Unsure of whether his teary eyes were real or not; I knew mine were.

Down the steps I walked, disappearing into the underground station where I swiped my metro card into the turnstile to hop onto a crowded train that would take me home, away from Pierre, and away from a love that didn't choose me... not on that day anyway.

Back inside my glamping suite, rain still poured down the windowpane in this humid jungle of condensed pressure. Isn't that what storms are made of? Extreme highs and lows that finally release from the clouds? Call it lightning, call it thunder, but even weather has a temperament of its own.

I closed my laptop and placed it on the nightstand beside the bed, and then pulled down the lamp string, turning off the lights.

Laying on my backside in complete darkness, I thought perhaps the one thing I didn't lose on that cold Winter's Day was the courage to live in my truth, even if that meant losing someone who wasn't ready to live in theirs. Besides, it wasn't the first time I'd been disappointed. Whether it was Mike drowning in alcohol or Pierre falling into confusion, they both taught me how to love someone and still let them go – because I too, deserved a healthy love.

And that was ok. Little did I know that as my journey continued, my North Star was about to take me way further than any NYC train could ever reach, so long as my destination wouldn't end on that stormy night in Tulum, Mexico.

Chapter 3

You Can Marry Anyone. Make Sure They Fan Your Flames for A Brighter Spark

W hoever said there was light at the end of the tunnel must've been an angel privileged to the divine secrets of creation. I couldn't believe how beautiful the sun shined the following day after the horrific storm that roared through Tulum the night before. It's as if the rain had ruined nothing, only fertilizing everything in its habitat for an auxiliary glow.

Talk about Paradise.

An all-inclusive breakfast was part of my package deal, and I had every intention of eating my freshly cooked strawberry-covered pancakes with a side of granola-glazed yogurt at the Tiki Hut's outdoor seating. Accompanying me were friendly little lizards climbing up and down the bamboo chairs and tables; some of them noticeably green, others camouflaging into the sand. I didn't mind sharing the atmosphere with these hot-blooded, long-tailed creatures that hopped around their home. For I was the one who was a guest in theirs.

Mexico, a country not too far from North America and yet another world away, seemed genuinely friendlier than the New York hustle I'd just left behind. Now that the storm had officially passed, my fear dissipated, allowing me to enjoy my foreign experience.

"Pssss... Take a look," said the waiter, walking up to my table. He pointed towards the iguana crawling amidst the rock-pebbled floor, not more than a few feet away.

"Hey, aren't you the hotel manager?" I asked, looking up from my seat.

He giggled. "I told you the sun would come out today. Y ahora, se puedes comer afuera."

I laughed along. "Yeah, you were right. I had nothing to fear, pero, tu sabes, it's a new environment for me," I said, looking down at my open-toe sandals, worried if an iguana or some insect would bite my feet below the table.

He kept smiling. "Quires algo para tomar?"

"Si... jugo, por favor," I replied. "Con un baso de café con leche. Muchas gracias."

After he turned and left, I enjoyed cutting into my pancakes at my little outdoor table that sat underneath a comfortable shade of palm trees. To say that I was basking in good vibes was an understatement. With each bite, I savored the juicy pancake syrup as I bird-watched a crew of chirping parakeets amid high tree branches, fascinated by what they could be saying.

After my meal, I returned to my room to change clothes.

Uncertain of what to wear, I played with my hair in the bathroom mirror, deciding on whether to leave it up or down in this tortured humidity, until finally letting my messy curls fall over my bare shoulders. I was on vacation, why stress? I slipped on one of my favorite spaghetti strap dresses and then popped in a pair of long, feathered earrings. Alas, I couldn't wait to hit the town.

After turning my number 11 keychain to lock the door behind me, I headed toward the main avenue and casually walked in and out of trendy bars and restaurants. Thank God I wore flat sandals because as sexy as this exotic land was, there was nothing but rocky, pebbled, dirt roads to get you around.

"You lost?" A construction worker asked, shoveling gravel.

I turned around. "No. Just enjoying the day."

"If you need help, let us know."

"Gracias," I smiled, secretly nervous about sticking out as a tourist.

Relax, I told myself. Plenty of women travel solo.

The funny thing is that if I wanted to blend in as a local, I failed miserably when my eyes lit up from the bohemian-themed shopping center I'd just approached. Such an American girl, I was ready to max out my credit card as I ran inside one of the boutiques.

What to wear? What to wear? I thought, excitedly looking through clothing racks, admiring every unique linen fabric dress hung amid matching bamboo hangers. I was in earth-tone heaven.

"I like your bracelets," a saleswoman complimented.

"You speak English?" I smiled.

"Un poquito pero, most of us do."

"That makes sense. Puerto Rico's like that too." I kept sliding hangers aside.

"Ahhh... Eres de Puerto Rico?"

"Yes," I answered. "Hey, how much is this?" I pulled out a long, white sundress from the rack.

She flipped the price tag around. "Son, 3,000 MXN pesos, pero that's $150 US dollars."

"Wow. That's a big difference," I said.

"Yea, it's a big difference; that's why we make good money from tourism. Estoy contento aqui," she admitted. "Pruebate."

"I think I will. Something about this white dress is different."

When I switched out of my green dress and into the white one, I looked into the fitting room mirror noticing how peaceful this lightweight garment felt on my body. It was as if the wind could blow right through my skin and clean up the cobwebs of my spirit. Albeit, it even matched my feather earrings, reminding me of why brides wear white on their wedding day.

I sighed... "I'll take it! I wanted a dress like this."

The saleswoman walked behind the registrar and smiled as she punched in the price.

I smiled back.

It was a good buy.

Back at my #11 hotel room, I knew exactly which man I'd write about next. I spread the white dress across the bed and thought of the time I met Kevin, the US Army Veteran-turned NJ sheriff that would whisk me off my feet only to drop me like a hot potato without any rhyme or reason after a few months of dating. Yep, he was the one I'd write about. Not because I held any grudges for how he left, but because I hadn't realized just how much the state of the world could impact who you date, despite thinking that romantic relationships are supposed to be a personal thing.

However, I learned quickly that the constellations in the sky had a different destiny planned for us little humans here on earth.

And what may that destiny be?

I remember swiping right on Kevin's Bumble profile. There was something heartfelt about his smile; not forced or fake but very genuine. The fact that he was 6-foot tall with a husky physique didn't hurt either. But, if I would've swiped left, we never would've met. That's how powerful one decision can be: an opened door for meeting a new soul, or a closed door for never knowing what could've been.

Good thing, we said hi.

When he drove to my house for the first time from New Jersey, I opened my door and squinted my eyes, "You look familiar." We both agreed. It could've been because he was of Italian descent working for law enforcement like my stepfather did, but for him, I'm not sure what the familiarity was.

That day we drove for almost two hours talking about life, spirituality, and his travels worldwide as a US Army soldier. Obviously, it wasn't your typical dress-to-impress candlelight dinner date. Still, I enjoyed the comfort of sitting in his warm temperature-controlled passenger seat, listening to him share stories of every foreign land he touched, including his favorite little beachy towns in Hawaii, Puerto Rico, and San Diego where he adopted a love for reggae music and a bit of booze. He seemed like such a laid-back guy, living peacefully like some Rastafarian trapped in a white man's body.

I guess I could understand his need for serenity since he fought in the Iraq war in the early 2000s. Assuming he must've felt conflicted about love and war as an American soldier, I felt his love for reggae possibly centered him whenever he'd turn up the radio volume. I considered him more of a protector than a killer, like a guardian angel fighting to defend the weaker which made it hard to imagine him in combat. Nevertheless, the irony of it all was that he was driving me to a Williamsburg pop-up shop so I could sell my new handmade candle collection; a spiritual based business I launched after moonlighting out of the music industry.

"What made you decide to make candles?" Kevin asked when turning the steering wheel.

"I was a Singer... Actually, I still am a Singer. Umm... To be honest, these days, I don't know because I haven't been performing like I used to, but since I already have a following, which is half the battle, I figured candle making was a cool venture. Plus, candles and aromatherapy... all that stuff soothes me. And... the candleflames... those little sparks remind me of the light within people."

He chuckled. "Not everyone is made of light, sweetie."

I tilted my head. "You've been to war. I can see why you'd say that, but let's just say, the light represents our inner spirit that's hidden beneath our outer shell of darkness."

He smirked. "Hmmm... Makes sense. How are sales? You make good money?" He pressed his foot on the gas as we drove through a series of green lights.

I laughed. "People always ask me that when it comes to business, but you know, it's not always about money. It's just something that fulfills me."

He turned on the car radio, switching it to a reggae station. Could this be Love? By Bob Marley played.

"I'm curious. What made you become a Cop?"

"You mean Sheriff?" He smiled, showing off his pearly whites.

"Yea."

He giggled. "I'm kidding. It's the same thing."

"Well, I'm just surprised a person like you would become a Cop," I smirked. "It's such a violent job. I mean, just imagine locking someone behind bars and then throwing away the key. Yea, bad people do bad shit, but that's not the kind of energy exchange I'd wanna be around... and then you jam out to Bob Marley, drinking a cool beer?"

He laughed again. "Ha, ha. You see, just like everyone always questions if whether or not you make money selling candles, everyone always asks me why I became a cop."

"You make a good point," I admitted. "Go on... I'm listening."

He shrugged his shoulders. "The truth is, I didn't know what the hell I was gonna do after leaving the military. I got comfortable traveling the world, and one of the best things it taught me was to pick a good place to retire in. Luckily for me, the experience gave me options. One of them was San Diego because it's laid-back with, like, no crime. So, I looked into becoming a Sheriff because I knew that with my military background, it would be a pretty easy transition."

"Ahhhh... San Diego... See that makes sense. It fits your personality."

"Exactly!" He emphasized. "I would've been patrolling the beach all day, not having to arrest a single soul because San Diego is one of the safest places. You see, the thing about being a cop is that it depends on the area you work in. I mean, who wouldn't wanna retire on a gig like that? Collecting overtime paychecks?! Shit, that would've been the life."

"So, what happened?"

"I was married... And my wife wanted to stay in Jersey to be closer to her family."

"I see..." I looked out the car window, thinking I must've dodged a bullet by not getting married young. Too many couples I knew gave up a life they really wanted by compromising on a mediocre one ending in divorce. Not that all marriages are mediocre – Of course not. But they're not for everyone. Yet, too many people buy into the hype of leaping into the ultimate commitment before committing to themselves.

Throughout the entire drive, he shared stories of his travels and insisted that more people should join the army because it would open their eyes to the world. According to him, it was the best decision he'd ever made. I felt conflicted because I had just recently started a new day job with an international humanitarian company where I befriended coworkers who were once Afghanistan and Iraq refugees – the same cultures he'd been at war with. And yet, all he listened to was reggae song after reggae song, with each song serving as his own personal musical therapy session or sound healing journey.

What were the odds?

Selling candles made me feel like I'd slipped out of a third-world dimension to enter the fifth because the light represented a higher truth. Something far bigger than playing victim or hero, but rather alien. I guess we all have that one thing that brings us peace outside of a secure paycheck. For me, it had started with a decade-long music career before I jumped into the DIY candle making market.

When pulling up to the flea market to park his car, Kevin had a surprise waiting for me and told me to open his glove department. When I did, my heart dropped.

There was a black gun.

Giggling, he told me not to fear. "I just wanted you to know I carry my pistol everywhere I go."

"What the fuck?" I whispered under my breath. "I don't know if I like this?"

"That's why I wanted you to see. I need to know if you're ok with it because I always carry it. It's just shocking right now because you're not used to seeing it."

I took a deep breath as I knew this was definitely a *new thing* for me because prior to dating Kevin, I never dated a cop before. And despite having grown up with a stepfather who retired from the force, I never – *never* – saw a gun in the house.

Once inside, Kevin helped me unpack my products to build my candle pop-up table display. I couldn't imagine him pointing a gun at someone, aiming to shoot to kill. But it was nice to have a protector, someone I could run to if I were ever in trouble. Lord knew how many incidents I could've avoided if certain people had known not to mess with me. After all, isn't that just one of the many reasons it's nice to have a man?

One of my favorite Indian Proverbs is, "A Woman's highest calling is to lead a man to his soul and unite him with source. A man's highest calling is to protect a woman, so she is free to walk the earth unharmed."

Unfortunately, too many worldwide reports of domestic violence ranging from rape, abuse, and infidelity have caused more than enough women to distrust men. And this once beautiful Indian proverb created with the intention for humanity to hold one another in reverence, has gone amiss.

Did Kevin and I have a future together? Would he protect me, not only physically but emotionally and spiritually too? After everything I'd been through with men, it took a lot for me to still believe I could actually trust someone and not have to worry about some deep dark secret suddenly flipping my world upside down like it did with Mike, or that some other woman could come in between our connection like it did with Pierre. Could Kevin actually be a good man? Someone I could rely on? We had yet to see, but as he reached into my bags to help me unpack my candle products, I felt this was a start.

~ ~

Superbowl Sunday was approaching and despite never having been a real sports fan, I joined Kevin's enthusiasm to watch J.Lo and Shakira's halftime performance. There was no way I was going to miss my girls on the biggest night of the year! Plus, I was happy that Kevin and I were planning future dates – it all seemed to be working out.

Throughout my workday, he'd check in with "Thinking of you" texts and "How's your day going?" I even got used to seeing his name appear across my iPhone the minute I'd walk through the door with an incoming Facetime. It was quickly becoming my favorite part of the day.

I vaguely remember it being either a Tuesday or Wednesday, sometime midweek when I'd been expecting Kevin's call to plan our upcoming Superbowl date. But as soon as I was about to swipe, *hello*, on that little green button, my heart sank.

It was Pierre.

Do I answer or let it go to voicemail? I thought. Quick! He might not call again! I answered, "Hello."

"Hey, beautiful. How are you?"

Memories flashed through my mind, sending signals down my nervous system of how it felt to be in love.

"I'm good," I leaned back against my kitchen counter, trying to hold myself up from shock. "It's nice to hear your voice, but it's been over a year since we last spoke. What made you call?"

"I never really forgot you, Jazz. You're not the type of person someone forgets."

"Can I ask an obvious question?"

He chuckled. "What's that?"

"Did you break up with Rebecca?"

I heard him take a deep breath. "I knew you'd ask that. Yea, we broke up a long time ago. I actually got into a whole other relationship with someone else."

Once again, I felt a punch to my gut the same way I felt the weekend he went to watch *Black Panther* with her.

My voice cracked, "You mean, I... I wasn't the first person on your mind to call when... umm, when you first broke up? I had thought she was the only thing standing in our way."

"Honestly, I was afraid to call you again," he confessed. "I never met anyone who –

"Hold, hold, hold on, Pierre. My phone is ringing on the other line."

"Oh, OK, no problem. Just call me back when you get a chance."

"Will do. Xo."

I quickly slid the green icon to the right and answered Kevin's facetime. That smile of his always brightened my mood.

"Hey babe," I greeted him.

I noticed his joyous expression slightly change into concern. "Hey, you ok?"

"Yea, of course I am."

"You seem a little skittish."

I was shocked. How the hell did he know something was off? I don't know why, but I felt compelled to share the truth, not wanting to begin a potential relationship with little white lies.

"Someone I used to date just called out of the blue," I confessed. "I literally haven't heard from him in over a year and a half, so it just threw me off a bit. That's all."

Obviously, Kevin wasn't too thrilled about the phone call, asking me what he wanted after so much time had passed. I told him that I was just as shocked as he was and assured him that it was nothing.

We continued our daily one-hour conversation as he flipped through paperwork in the office, pausing every now and then whenever an emergency came through his body-attached radio speaker.

At first, it was a little disturbing to hear how much crime he'd deal with on a regular basis, but in retrospect, it wasn't as bad as hearing some of the third-world horror stories at my humanitarian job. Whether I went to lunch or met for happy hour, some of my coworker's shared stories of relatives beheaded in Iraq from trying to escape radical religious groups, witnessing their pets being shot on sight, and other horrific experiences too painful to imagine.

It was apparent that regardless of what part of the globe we talked about, the nature of duality coexisted on every land, some more extreme than others. As far as I knew, there was no utopian place untouched by darkness.

Before Kevin and I hung up the phone, we made plans to watch Superbowl Sunday at my place that coming weekend – just us two for our own private party. As crazy as life can get with all its ups and downs, it was important to celebrate the high moments whenever we could.

"Whoa!" I screeched, popping open a bottle of champagne. Kevin and I toasted in my kitchen before moving over to my living room.

Ruby red hourglass-shaped dancers shook their asses on the world's largest stage to Shakira's opening performance. All twenty-something of them surrounding the Pop Star as she cat-walked down the center aisle with microphone in hand, commanding the audience's attention in a nighttime event where bright spotlights followed her every move.

I turned to see Kevin's reaction, whose eyes were glued to the TV. Who could blame him? Shakira whipped out a thick rope, holding both edges in a seductive stance of sexual bondage as she swerved her curvy hips side to side. She then lifted her arm straight into the air and spun her rope around in true cowgirl fashion, flipping her long, dirty blonde hair over her right eye singing her hit song, "*Whenever – Wherever*."

It was less than three minutes into the show, and I was already getting up from my couch to cheer on my girl! Fireworks dispersed into the air, sending off a larger-than-life celebration into the homes of millions of worldwide viewers. And yet, it was only the beginning.

Beyond the handheld concert glowsticks amid the front row, cameras glided up towards the 50-year-old Latin sensation, Jennifer Lopez, capturing her perfectly fit body sliding down a stripper pole in a skintight black leather catsuit. It was no surprise to be mesmerized by her beauty amidst flashing lights, but what really caught everyone off guard was the surprise introduction of her eleven-year-old daughter, Emme, who began singing, "*If you wanna live your life, live it all the way and don't you waste it.*"

I can't lie, I got teary-eyed. She looked adorable performing alongside an entire choir of kids as her mother walked beside her, unveiling a cape with the Puerto Rican flag on one side and the American flag on the other.

I was so proud, I could've fainted. Kevin laughed at me in good humor, the two of us drinking our champagne while bopping our shoulders to the beat. It ended with these two powerhouses, Shakira and J.Lo, dancing salsa until they both gave one last smile amid their legendary performance.

Coincidently, Kevin and I both received texts at the same time from our mothers.

Mine's read, "Wasn't that the most awesome show you've ever seen!? I've never been prouder to be a Latina in my entire life. They are my hero's!"

Kevin wouldn't read what his mother wrote.

"What'd she say?" I asked.

He waved his hands as if to brush it off.

"Tell me, what'd she say?" I insisted.

"She thought it was good."

"You're lying. What did she really say?"

He shrugged his shoulders, "She thought it was a little too much for halftime."

Another text came in and they kept communicating, but I didn't want to keep investigating because it was his mother, and she was entitled to her opinion.

I wondered why his marriage really didn't work; I thought as I came back to myself in the hotel room. Looking at the white dress spread out in front of me, I wondered if his mother had any influence over their divorce or if Kevin just fell out of love? There I was in Mexico, remembering that Kevin's ex-wife was, in fact, Mexican. They had bi-racial kids whom I'd never gotten the chance to meet, but it was nice to know that some couples saw beyond their ethnicities when getting together.

That whole time of dating Kevin was back in the beginning of 2020 – the year that Shakira and J.Lo's performance meant more than entertainment because they wanted to send a message about sex trafficking across Latin America. I'm not sure if it did the trick, but in show business, Artists had to maneuver their messages very subtly not to offend fans. I even remember the Trump meme trending Instagram, *"Shakira and J.Lo can stay!"* The joke, born out of halftime's greatest show, melted some of the tension around the Mexican border-wall controversy because that's how influential these two powerhouse Latinas were.

I sat on the edge of my bed, realizing how much privilege I had as an American citizen touring Mexico because I could afford to splurge money like a Queen. In fact, I was even treated better than the locals just because of the mere fact that tourists drive so much business into their country.

Outside my window, the sun was setting amidst hanging garden lights that turned on around 8pm. Since the night was still young, I decided to put on my new white dress and grab a cerveza at the neighboring bar. When turning the doorknob to leave, I heard a man's voice introducing a live band on the microphone and then noticed a little frog hopping passed my feet, entering the room.

"Ahhh, such a good omen," I smile to myself. Legend has it that frogs approaching someone's doorstep are a sign of good luck and transformation, confirming that this trip was becoming more of a blessing than I thought. I let the frog hop inside my room and lock the door behind me.

To the sounds of Stevie Wonder's lyrics, I could hear the band member singing nearby, *"And maybe too, if you would believe, you too might be, overjoyed, over loved, over me..."*

I sang along, loving how the song permeated through tropical air with good vibes. Frogs, music, and sunsets, I was proud of myself for choosing to venture into what seemed to transpire into a self-healing honeymoon. And let's be honest. Music never left my system – it was just giving me room to breathe and rebalance my spirit during this self-reflecting journey.

Chapter 4
The Only Thing Guaranteed in Life Is Change

It wasn't over between me and Pierre. I should've known the day I answered his call and reopened that electric current. Our chord hadn't been fully cut.

"You're dating a fuck'n white cop!?" Pierre challenged.

"You're lucky I even picked up the phone after the way you disappeared almost two years ago!" I told him.

"A fuck'n white cop!?" He continued. *"Bad boys, bad boys, what you gonna do? What you gonna do when they come for you?"* He sarcastically teased.

I rolled my eyes, realizing that the heartbreak I had endured must've been for my highest good because I was so turned off by his immaturity.

"Big fuck'n deal, he's white. You don't even know him." I paced back and forth in my kitchen, talking to Pierre over the phone because our conversation had gotten interrupted by Kevin the other day.

"Do you love this guy?" Pierre asked.

I opened my refrigerator door in search of food. "I mean... It's still new," I replied, pulling out two slices of wheat bread and a stick of butter. "But I really like him, and I think it can actually go somewhere."

Pierre laughed. "Girl, please. You know you still belong to me. We fell in love the first day we met."

"Yea, you're right. We fell in love fast, but you still picked someone else over me." I pushed two slices of bread down into my toaster.

I heard him pressing the button on a juice machine, making a health shake in his kitchen too. The both of us ended up enjoying a casual afternoon at home in our separate apartments, whipping up something to eat as we chit chatted over the phone about life's challenges – the good, the bad, and the ugly. Our conversation flowed as if no time had passed. As always, we clicked like besties.

Interrupted once again, an incoming call rang from Kevin.

"Pierre, I have to let you go. I'll call you back later."

"Wait. What!? Is it that white cop calling again? *Bad boys, bad boys, what you gon' do?*"

"Oh stop!" I teased back. "For real. I have to go."

"No, no, no, make him wait! If he's really into you, he'll call back."

"I'm not gonna play games with him. We're too old for that."

"Nah, fuck that. Test him." Pierre challenged.

And he won, because the phone stopped ringing on the other line. I sighed. "Uh oh. I hope I don't fuck things up with this guy."

"Ha, ha! Why?!" He chuckled. "Because you didn't pick up immediately?"

"Not exactly. It's because our routine is off, so now I have to make something up."

"Just tell him you were taking a shit, my god."

"Wow, you're such a good liar that it literally scares the SHIT out of me."

We both laughed.

Eventually, however, we did hang up, and I called Kevin back to learn that he had bought us tickets to a New Jersey Nets basketball game at Madison Square Garden for Valentine's week.

What were the odds that Pierre reentered my life during the same season he had left two years ago? I remembered everything as if it were yesterday, in the middle of Winter, specifically around the holiday of love when he took Rebecca to watch *Black Panther*. I, instead, ended up watching *Fifty Shades of Grey* alone on Netflix, romanticizing over two fictional characters who didn't even exist; they were merely two Actors on a screen entertaining me. But this was real life and Pierre was back.

Was this a second chance for us to work things out? Was it karma? Or was this just a repeated lesson I failed to learn before?

For the next few days, Kevin wasn't calling as much as he did. I was confused. Could he pick up on the fact that Pierre and I had reconnected over the phone? I couldn't understand why he wasn't texting, "I miss you," anymore? It was more like breadcrumbing, leaving just enough to string me along.

At work, I stared at my phone. And when his texts didn't come, I'd text him first. He'd reply, but I didn't like that now I was the one chasing him because if I didn't, I feared he'd start seeing someone else – or maybe he already was seeing someone else, and I just didn't know it. I never considered New Jersey to be a long-distance problem until realizing he could've searched for someone more local. Afterall, we met on a dating app! What was stopping him from finding someone else through the path of least resistance – *a swipe!?*

Valentine's Day was approaching when Kevin kept his promise by bringing me to Madison Square Garden that Friday, but his body language was completely off. Our hello kiss felt so aloof that it made me wonder if he'd slept with someone else. It was as if the happy-go-lucky, reggae-listening, "potential boyfriend," was just a dream – or a fling.

In the spirit of basketball, I pretended to enjoy the game and whenever one of the players made a slam dunk, I cheered. When the ushers came around, Kevin still did the manly thing of ordering us concession food. We ate, we talked, we laughed. But he wasn't fully present, as if his mind were elsewhere. I asked if he was ok and eventually, he confessed.

"I have a bad feeling about driving into New York," he told me.

I cocked my head. "Why? You drive into New York all the time."

He took a sip of soda. "Yea, but I have this bad feeling. I don't know why? It's not you. I just feel like I shouldn't come into the city anymore. You can come to New Jersey whenever you want, but you don't have a car."

"I don't mind coming to New Jersey. It's nice to get away. But are you sure that's all it is?"

He took another sip before placing his soda back on the floor. "I don't know how long this is gonna last? You coming to Jersey all the time? You won't get tired of that?"

I started to feel like he was making excuses to get rid of me by letting me down slowly. Just as I thought. He probably met someone conveniently local. I looked down at the floor, feeling disappointed. The row in front of us stood up, cheering the game. When I looked back at Kevin, he stood up too, cheering the winning team.

The stadium began chanting, *"We Will, We Will Rock You!"* But I silently stayed frozen growing a lump inside my throat, trying not to cry. Out of all the weekends that another breakup could take place, why did it have to be Valentine's, again?

Maybe I was getting ahead of myself, but I just felt like the only reason he brought me to the game was to keep his promise. Still, I felt it coming, the discard – with the excuse that I lived too far. Even though it wasn't too far for him when we had sex on super bowl Sunday. Yea, I left that part out.

The crowd continued chanting while I wanted to quietly disappear, wondering who the other woman was? But I didn't want to ruin our night with my insecurities, so I kept my thoughts to myself as my throat tightened.

Eventually, he noticed. "You ok?"

I looked up, without making a peep.

He sat back down. "You don't like the game?"

I slightly rolled my eyes. "You just told me you don't like coming into NY... I'm worried this might be the last time we ever see each other."

He frowned as if feeling guilty for hurting me. "Hey, aren't you still friends with your ex?"

"Seriously? Is that the reason you're distancing yourself from me?"

"No, Jasmine. It's not. I honestly have a bad feeling about NY. I don't know what it is, but something in my gut repulses me from coming here. It's not you. It's just the energy of this city. It's like, bad vibes or something."

"How is that even possible?" I asked, eyebrows arched. "You fought in the desert storm Gulf War, but Manhattan scares you?"

He chuckled, turning his body toward me to get a better look into my eyes.

"Why don't you see your ex since he lives in NY, too?" He asked.

I wanted to ask so bad if he'd found someone else in New Jersey. I just didn't have the courage to speak because I was too afraid to find out.

"Why would you push me back to my ex-boyfriend?" I asked.

"It would be easier, Jazz. You shouldn't have to troop all the way to New Jersey just to see me."

"But what if I want to?"

"Excuse me," a woman said, walking through our row to leave the stadium. Behind her was a gang of people ready to leave. It was our sign that our night was coming to an end, and it was time to go home. But I didn't look forward to saying goodbye because I was doubtful if we'd ever say hello again.

"He left you?" Pierre asked. "What a jerk."

"Why's he a jerk? You did the same thing. You ghosted."

"That was different."

I almost dropped my cell phone from disbelief. "How in the world was it different?"

"Meet me in the city and we'll talk about it. It's officially Valentine's Day. You shouldn't be alone."

I always looked into the deeper meaning of signs and coincidences. It was Valentine's Day for crying out loud, and out of all the people in the world, I ended up with Pierre at a crowded bar on the lower east side, downing vodka shots as we vented about our ex's, laughing and crying like two drunk besties chanting to Jay Z and Beyonce's song *Me and My Girlfriend.*

Eyes slanted from too much alcohol in his system, he sang, *"So let's lock this down like it's supposed to be. The '03 Bonnie and Clyde: Hov' and B holla! All I need in this life of sin, is me and my girlfriend."* I joined the chorus, *"Down to ride 'til the very end, is me and my boyfriend (me and my boyfriend)."*

Pierre gently placed my left hand on top of his. "You're gonna be my wife one day, Jazz."

"I want a black diamond ring," I chuckled.

"I'm serious," he looked into my eyes. "You're my best friend."

I leaned my head into his chest, feeling as if our relationship had deepened overtime. And with our fingers interlaced, I couldn't help but notice how similar our caramel complexion was as if we were both born from the same cinnamon tone, like real siblings – possibly from another lifetime, of course.

I began to feel the way I did on that Winter's Day at battery park, when all we had was our body warmth to keep us comfortable by the water. He sure was my best friend; here we were, two drunk fools sharing our past experiences with lovers who came and went, while the two of us remained.

Before the night was over, Pierre asked me to go back to his uptown apartment, I suppose to rekindle the magic on Valentine's Day. But remembering how Pierre had chosen another woman over me, I didn't want to risk becoming emotionally vulnerable again. Having our friendship repaired meant the world to me and I didn't want to ruin that. Instead, I headed back into the subway, just like I'd done on the day he'd chosen Rebecca over me. But this time, Rebecca was no longer a part of his life, and yet, I still was.

~❖~

Over the next few weeks, I had gotten no word from Kevin – just as I had thought. Our basketball date had been the last time we ever saw each other, even though he didn't break up with me. He only said he was growing tired of driving into NY, but never said it was over. I sent him texts and voice notes to touch base but got no word. *Zero. Nothing. Natha. Zelch.* I even went so far as to film a one-minute phone clip of myself talking and sent it to him. Desperate times call for desperate measures. Sure, I was embarrassed, but I also felt disrespected by his lack of compassion for a decent goodbye.

Was I that foolish for believing we had feelings for each other? We had sex which was intimate for me at this stage of my life. I wasn't some 21-year-old College student with raging hormones, desiring sex just for fun and exploration. I was a 38-year-old woman in tune with her feminine flow, looking to connect deeply with a man for substance and love. But I guess, it meant nothing to him. Either that, or he had found someone else. I wish he would've given me some closure because being ignored was pure torture.

I never thought I'd say it, but thank God Pierre was around to soften the blow. He'd reach out, asking to meet in the city for late night comedy shows and drinks at the billiards to score some games of pool. It was nice being pursued by Pierre after the way we ended things in the past, but I was beginning not to trust men as a species. Yea, I said it. Did they just want what they couldn't have? Would Pierre leave me again if I satisfied him with the reward after the hunt?

All I knew is that being friends with Pierre felt safe and comforting, as long as we didn't cross the line. But then again, I had a lot of male friends. Especially, back at work where my male coworkers were some of the coolest to talk to. And, the best part, is that I never had to worry about a broken heart because as professionals, we had shared so much mutual respect – aside from a side wink, here and there.

As the days passed, Monday through Friday, Pierre's texts gradually replaced Kevin's throughout the day. It was nice, developing this new friendship that I never thought in a million years would've resurrected. God really surprised us.

"Hey, Jazz. The company is closing down for the next two weeks, so take whatever you need to take home because the building will be locked."

"What!?" My eyebrows arched, looking up at my manager from my office desk.

"Oh, you didn't hear?" He looked confused.

"Hear what!?" I was even more confused.

He rolled up his sleeves to chit-chat. "Where have you been all this time?"

"What are you talking about?"

"Jazz, there's a virus that's been spreading all over NYC. We're a humanitarian company, so you know we gotta be on top of things like this."

"Oh wow, it's that bad?"

"Go pack your things and leave; none of us are staying. We'll mail you a laptop so you can work from home."

I smiled. "Say no more! I love the work-from-home part!" I giggled, not understanding yet what was in store for the near future. Although I must admit, even though he said we'd be gone for only two weeks, I looked at my desk and had this strong feeling I might not ever work there again. And so, I emptied out my desk taking all my belongings and whispered a gentle goodbye to one of the best companies I had ever worked for because somehow, I just knew, that this was going to be the start of something way bigger than any of us could ever imagine.

Once I made it down the elevator and into the lobby, I called Pierre, excited to tell him about my new mini vacation. It turned out to be an invitation to stay at his place for the next few days, which meant that I'd be staying in Harlem instead of Brooklyn.

"When I get home after work, we'll go to the grocery store and buy all the supplies we'll need for the entire week," Pierre said. "We'll get gloves, hand sanitizers, masks, and buy as much food as possible. Nah, fuck that, I'M STUFFING MY ENTIRE REFRIGERATOR FOR AN ENTIRE MONTH!"

"Wait, why are you going overboard? Isn't this only supposed to be like a two-week thing?"

"Jazz, have you been watching the news? This disease is about to spread like wildfire!"

"You mean, like the Zombie apocalypse or something?"

"Yes, exactly like that! Yo! This shit ain't no joke! I'm about to buy some weapons too because when all these stores shut down, the hood gonna get live!"

My Irish-Norwegian Viking look-alike, ex-boyfriend, Mike's image suddenly popped into my mind. *Holy mother of God*, I thought. *All those apocalyptic shows he made me watch, telling me I better prepare because one day it'll be real. The fall of civilization. I think it's happening.*

Chapter 5
At The Heart of The Matter, Love is Peace

It was the middle of the week when my cousin, Linda, finally flew into Mexico. "I'm so excited!" She exasperated over the phone. "I'm going to take you to the cenote, to the beach parties, and maybe we can even swim with the mermaids!"

"Whoa! I don't know about swimming with mermaids. That's like snorkeling. I'm afraid of the deep sea."

"Oh, it's nothing. My friend does it for a living and she'll teach you. She's a mermaid coach. I'll send you her Instagram so you can see her underwater pictures."

"Hmmm... We'll see," I confessed.

"Girl, don't be such a chicken shit. You didn't come all the way to Mexico to stay on the same strip the whole time. You have to explore."

"I am exploring. I'm in Mexico!"

She giggled over the phone. "Ok, well, I know which glamping hotel you're staying at, so I'll be there in an hour. Get ready to come out of your comfort zone!"

Too late. I was panicking. The thought of swimming in the ocean frightened me. I didn't mind swimming close to shore, but the idea of going deep wasn't my thing, especially after experiencing that tropical storm the other night. I was no fan of taking risks. But before I knew it, Linda, was at my door, all curly haired out at 5 foot 4, smiling from ear to ear.

"Hiiiii!" She threw her arms around me, hugging me tightly. We had never gone on vacation together, let alone, saw each other outside of special occasions and holidays. So, this was a real treat to be able to bond with my cousin without other relatives. Just Linda, and myself.

We started our day by visiting a row of rusty old 80's style bikes stacked against a jungle Jaguar wall mural. If wildcats roaming Mexico wasn't dangerous enough, then riding one of these broken-down bikes surely would be.

"Are you kidding? This is what we're working with?" I asked. I slid my hand across one of the hardened flat seats. "How's my ass supposed to sit on this?"

Linda laughed. "Stop being so paranoid. Just choose your favorite color and ride it."

"On these rocks? Wait! You can't ride that fast. You'll fall!"

Linda sped off yelling for me to catch up. "I'm not waiting for you! I told you I'm gonna take you out of your comfort zone!"

I leaped on top of a thin baby blue bike and pushed the pedals as hard as I could, trying to catch up to my cousin who blissfully led the way.

As we rode our bikes onto a narrow street, cars drove past us on the left, and the ocean waves crashed next to us on the right. One bad move, and you could fall to your death. I was sweating bullets from my forehead, afraid of getting into an accident as other bikers joyfully rode passed us with hair blowing in the wind. Every now and then, my cousin would yell, "Are you ok back there? You seem quiet!"

"I'm alive! I'm alive!" I'd reply.

But I couldn't help but notice how the sky was darkening, the same way it did on the first day of my arrival. "Linda!" I yelled. "I'm not sure how far we should go because it looks like a storm is coming!"

"It always rains, Jazzy! You can't let that stop you. It's just nature."

"Yea but riding a bicycle against traffic in the rain doesn't seem safe."

Linda kept riding. "If it rains too hard, we'll stop. But a little bit of rain is fine. Just push through the fear!"

And, so, we kept riding our bicycles through tropical streets, sightseeing garden cafes amid palm trees as Linda pointed towards yoga studios and holistic spas along the way. "Oh Jazzy, you would love that place! And that one, too! And that one!"

All I knew was that as each rain drop hit my skin, my fear grew stronger and stronger. "Those places are my kinda vibe, but have you noticed that it's getting pretty dark?"

"Yea, it'll pass," Linda tried to assure me as she kept gleefully riding her bike.

"Well, honestly, I don't want us to get caught riding in a thunderstorm when we can look for shelter now."

"Let's just go a little further down the road, and then we'll stop."

"Noooo! I really think we should stop now. I'm telling you, the sky is gonna open up! And these storms are way more powerful than the ones back home."

"Ok fine," Linda finally relented as we rode into a nearby café, driving underneath its heart shaped roof showering us with a stream of rain as we entered.

"Look! It's a sign!" I said, pointing at the water falling from the center dip of the heart. My cousin smirked. "Yea, I guess it is. But as soon as the rain stops, we're gonna keep riding all the way!"

I saw her spaghetti strap falling off her shoulder and lifted it back up.

"Hey! Don't do that!" She ordered, cocking her head back.

"Why? I'm just trying to help."

"What? You don't like how I'm dressed?"

"I love how you're dressed! You've always had style! I just didn't think you noticed that your strap fell."

And then it hit me. She must've gotten defensive because our family is very conservative and they've always felt that as ladies, we need to present ourselves a certain way, especially if we wanted to be considered "wife material."

I knew the feeling. It was part of the reason I didn't visit my family that much and only saw Linda at special occasions. The conversations always turned into lectures about when we were going to settle down and start a family. "Your clock is ticking. If you don't choose someone soon, you'll miss your window of opportunity," our Abuelita would say. I'm sure my cousin loved her just as much as I did. We all loved her. But the patronizing speech wouldn't stop with our loving grandmother born from an older generation. (At least that we could understand). It came from literally everyone. And, regardless of their good intentions, we still felt criticized for not being the "ideal" female relative.

I looked my cousin in her eyes, "Hey, I honestly really like the way you dress. You've always looked amazing. And, I'm not just saying that to say it. Shit girl, I kind'a dress the same way! You know how I do." I winked.

She smiled back, and I can tell she believed me. Since we had never bonded before, I couldn't really blame her for being skeptical of me. Besides, I understood all too well how much pressure we have as women in society to be this or to be that. And when you come from a conservative Latin family like ours, the pressure for a woman to behave a certain way in a machismo world is intensified.

As we stood underneath the heart shaped rooftop, waiting for the storm to pass, a loud bang of thunder rumbled across the sky followed by golden strips of lightening. We ended up chit chatting about our love lives and how we lived it up in our 30's in the most unconventional ways. It was nice to speak to a relative, who, in many ways, walked a similar path as myself. In that regard, some of the pressure was off because we could just be ourselves.

So what? That we weren't yet married at our ages.

So what? That we didn't yet own houses because we rented.

And so, what? That we traveled solo without male companions.

Furthermore, our freedom granted us the opportunity to have an adventure in a foreign country that could last as long as we wanted it to, even if that meant extending our trip to travel as far across the globe as we'd like.

But in this instance, I wasn't moving too far after a truck splashed water all over us. My cousin giggled, "You ready to get back out there and ride to the cenote?"

I looked at her, fearfully. "I have to be honest... This weather isn't what I expected."

"Yea, but it stopped raining Jazzy. In climates like this, it always rains on and off."

"Nah.... I think I'd rather wait for a full day of sunshine just to be on the safe side."

She cupped both my hands and felt them trembling inside hers. "Oh my god. You really are scared. You're shaking."

I nodded my head yes. "I know myself. If the current gets a little too strong, it can pull me out to sea, and I might not be strong enough to swim towards a tree or grab onto something nearby. I know I'm thinking worst-case scenario, but I have my limits."

Linda looked disappointed, but didn't want to push too hard. We agreed that we'd ride back to my glamping hotel and have brunch in the beach resort. But first, we walked underneath the heart shaped rooftop, and then stopped to hug each other as the water cascaded over us. We said a little cleansing prayer, thanking Mother Earth for magnetizing us to this mysterious trip we both coincidently booked around the same time. It was just by chance, that both of us had the urge to travel to Tulum, Mexico on the same week without either of us preplanning it together. If that wasn't the universe sending us a divine wink, then I don't know what else to say! As far as I was concerned, something magical was in the air.

"You know, we're really not single." I told her, standing there in wet clothes and slippery sandals. "We're freeeeee!"

Linda let go and swung her arms into the air singing, "Mexico is my happy place!"

Something about her spirit shone through her eyes as she began dancing under pouring rain, lifting one leg up like a ballerina, gracefully welcoming an unpredictable storm with twists and turns of her own. Admiring her courage, I partnered with her, the two of us pouncing around in wet clothes.

To capture the moment, we had someone snap photos of us posing beneath the heart-shaped rooftop to remember where we had our first heart-to-heart as adult women who afterwards, allowed our inner child to dance in the rain. It reminded me of a time when I danced with Pierre, back in the concrete jungle of Harlem behind brick city walls. Sometimes, us grown folks need to let loose because no matter where someone is in their own book of life, the world can be full of drama.

Pierre was obsessed with googling the news on his cellphone to stay up-to-date with the coronavirus, and phone calls came in from our West Coast friends, all sharing stories of how schools, shopping malls, barbershops, gyms, museums, and basically the entire world was shutting down.

"Fuck all these stores closing. What about all them side chic's disappearing, leaving dudes stuck home with their miserable wives!? Now, dudes can't escape!" Pierre almost died laughing.

"That's just wrong," I told him.

After laughing too hard, Pierre caught his breath. "I'm joking, I'm joking," he sighed. "No, I'm not! Sike! Hahahaha!"

I rolled my eyes, knowing it was all in good fun. At least I knew that for the next few weeks, I wouldn't be bored.

In the living room, he played 80's R&B. We took cleaning supplies from his kitchen cabinets to completely redo his place since we'd be staying indoors for God only knew how long. Ajax, Comet, Palmolive – you name it, we had it. Sponges, rags, gloves, brooms, mops, we were prepared. It was like a battle of bacteria. We were going to clean every corner of that apartment until it smelled of fresh lavender candles and rosemary diffusers.

My hair was twisted up in a messy bun, ready for war as I scrubbed every dish in his overflooded sink. I was determined to smudge sage after all of this was over as Pierre emptied out his draws and threw tons of clothes, towels, pillowcases and blankets inside of three hefty laundry bags. Teamwork, we were good at that. But when New Edition's *"Cool It Now"* came on Alexa, we dropped what we were doing and ran into the living room, singing lyrics from the top of our lungs.

"Cool it now, you better slow it down. Ooooh watch out!" We sang. *"You're gonna lose control."*

Pierre broke out a Roger Rabbit, leaping midway into the air as if he were on a Kid N' Play *"House Party"* movie set. I spun around in a circle and did the running-man, transporting back into my Junior High School dance moves. I hadn't had that much fun in years; my hair a frizzy mess, falling all over my face. Yes, this is what working-from-home looked like.

After a full day of sweeping and mopping, and acting like two teenage besties, we walked into the bedroom to rest our heads, except that we were met with the sounds of banging pots and pans outside hundreds of windows.

"WTF?" I questioned.

"Yo, check that out!" Pierre smiled, running over to his fire escape. "Come over here. Look."

I followed him to the fire escape and witnessed a symphony of multicultural men, women and children sitting on their balconies and windowsills, celebrating the nurses who walked to the subway station after ending their 7:00pm hospital shifts.

"You're the real heroes of this epidemic!" Some cheered.

The diversity of New Yorkers ranged from Dominicans, Puerto Ricans, Jamaican's, Italians, West Indian's, African's, Arab Muslims, Jews and more. Every naked hand, in various shades of skin tones clapping, whistling and banging on hard skillets and cast-iron pans, anything for the sound to reach as far as possible, so that the nurses couldn't fail to notice how proud the people were of them.

"You see, this is why I love Harlem," Pierre smiled. He placed both arms out, leaning into the front rim of his fire escape. His black mala beaded bracelet shined in the sunset, the one piece of jewelry he never took off.

A saxophone player started blowing sweet sounds from the fourth-floor windowsill, horizontal to the left of us. The city that never sleeps was more than just awake that day, it was bursting with vibrancy as the musician held his golden "S" shaped instrument, slightly outside of his window sending rhythmic notes into the atmosphere.

It was such an incredible sight to see, the sun setting on that early Spring Day with rays of honey dripped sunlight beaming down the street, illuminating even the grayest of old rustic stained buildings. But unfortunately, there were also ambulances strolling up and down the streets, their sirens colliding with the harmonies of song to alarm everyone that more covid cases were being picked up around the clock. They parked in front of buildings, releasing paramedics into the homes of people who ended up in stretchers being transported to the nearest hospitals. It was a bittersweet memory to see people coming together to try and turn a morbid situation into an enlightening moment of wisdom – that when so much death is upon is, only the light of life can conquer darkness.

Later that evening, Pierre and I cuddled underneath the sheets, lying in bed while watching CNN before falling asleep. Images of thousands of caskets lined up throughout Italy filled the screen. They had one of the highest death tolls throughout the world, turning Covid from an epidemic into a pandemic. It was surreal to see how far Covid had spread, as if there was no place on Earth untouched by this plague. Eventually we shut off the TV and laid in the dark, snuggled next to each other, our warm bodies keeping each other comforted by the unknowns of tomorrow. As usual, Pierre turned on an R&B playlist to fall asleep to something soothing.

"If The World Was Ending" by JP Saxe and Julia Michaels came on.

"How'd they know to write a song like this?" Pierre whispered into the night. "No one knew the world would be like this a few months ago. Are you listening to these lyrics?"

If the world was ending, you'd come over right?
The sky'd be falling and I'd hold you tight
And there wouldn't be a reason why
We would even have to say goodbye

I smiled beneath the shadows, my heart happy to beat beside his. Pierre may have driven me crazy at times, but there wasn't any other soul I'd rather share those unprecedent moments with.

The next day, we walked outside and put on our cheaply made, thin blue cotton medical masks and took selfies kissing. No, we didn't feel each other's lips through the fabric and that was the whole joke. It was like tap kissing a ten-year-old after school. We both stretched the white rubber band around our earlobes to firmly hold the mask in place that honestly, suffocated me.

"I hate breathing into this stupid thing!" I complained.

"Yea, well you have to wear it, or you'll die!" He muzzled through the cotton fabric.

I rolled my eyes. "You really think this swanky thing is gonna protect us from a disease that is THAT CONTAGIOUS? I think we'd need a real gas mask, like the ones we actually don't have access to."

Pierre's eyes lit up. "Oh shit, we can order surgical masks before they're sold out! You're right. These are too thin! They got multilayered ones. Don't worry. I'll keep us safe, beauty."

I blushed. I loved how he snuck in the word, beauty.

It was all good for a couple of weeks. Since most stores were closed during Covid's quarantine, we'd walk hand in hand to the only opened date place in town: the supermarket, shopping for food and plants. Eventually, his apartment turned into a garden oasis as we brought back little house plants to decorate the space. Every morning, we took turns watering them by the window and watched them transforming from budding babies to blooming beauties. It was amazing how healing nature vibes could be regardless of how toxic the world was on the other side of apartment walls. When usually, it's the great outdoors that people run to, instead, our home became a paradise in the making.

Only, it really wasn't "our home," it was Pierre's, and I was merely a valued guest who would eventually return to my little sacred space back in Brooklyn, which was also a heavenly abode, I must say.

"My birthday's coming up, you know?" I reminded him.

"I know. I got you," he winked. "It's around Mother's Day, right?"

"You're close. It's in May, but not that soon. I'm a Gemini, remember? Sign of the twins."

Pierre shot a devilish smirk. "Oh yea, How can I forget? Gemini's are nothing but trouble."

My jaw dropped. "Seriously? You're gonna say that right now?"

Pierre giggled. "Yea, good trouble." He pumped the front of his crotch, sexualizing what he meant.

"You know you love me," I teased.

He leaned against the wall entrance of his bedroom, crossing one leg over the other in his baggy sweatpants and loose-fitting Tee. "I do love you, pretty girl."

He then turned around and walked over to his desktop, looking for a song to play. What do you know? It was our record, *"North Star."*

"I used to listen to this song all the time when I was by myself. And even though we had stopped speaking, I couldn't delete it."

"Whatever happened with you and Rebecca?" I asked. "You never explained how it ended."

"She left me."

"What!? After all that guilt, you were carrying!?"

Pierre arched his eyebrows, "Yeah, but she had every right to."

"Wow. You know my heart was torn to pieces when you chose her over me."

"I'm sorry Jazz. It was just a bad time in my life, and I was trying to do the right thing."

"I understand," I said, listening to Nina Simone's drumming in the background. "Maybe something bigger than you and I brought us back together, cause... look at us now."

Later that evening, I ordered an Uber back home to Brooklyn with a full spirit, feeling emotionally satisfied. But once I sat alone in the car, for some reason, I thought of Kevin-- the cop I used to date. I remembered him saying that he had a bad feeling about driving into NY. Maybe his intuition had been in touch with the pandemic during its inception behind the scenes – as if he knew something wasn't right within the universe.

Lockdown. Who would've thought?

As time moved on, I joined online company meetings, each of us taking turns to discuss when we thought we'd return to the office. Some said, "Two more weeks." Others said, "Not 'till Fall." I sarcastically said, "Probably never." We giggled.

"I wouldn't mind," said someone on the call.

"I'd work from the beach," said another.

I don't think any of us had ever realized just how much our bodies needed a break from the 9 to 5 hustle. We all shared stories about how much more productive we'd become by skipping our daily commutes, being able to roll out of bed and open our laptops still in pajamas. The amount of time we got back was invaluable; and none of us wanted to trade that up ever again.

When my birthday rolled around, Pierre, actually left Harlem to come to my side of town for a change, baring gifts for my special day. This was huge for Pierre because for him, traveling over that Brooklyn bridge was a world away.

When I opened my front door, he held a beautiful Lavender plant and pink orchid as an extension from his home to mine. I loved anything he gave me, but the best gift – the most surprising gift – and the most meaningful gift, were the sweatpants he bought me, which were the same ones he'd given me the night I slept over his place after recording *North Star.* It was like, I was never meant to leave because everything about us said, "home."

I was officially 39 years old; the last year of my 30's, time to say goodbye to one era of my life and begin another. Spending my special day with Pierre during Covid lockdown was the most chill vibe. Nothing fancy or over-the-top. Just him, myself, flowers, and love. But if I would've known what was about to happen the next day... Within 24 hours, everything changed.

"Turn on CNN! Now!" Pierre was already back home and had called me the next morning.

I picked up my remote control and pressed power. When I turned on the news, they replayed a video of an African American man named George Floyd being suffocated by a police officer kneeling on his neck. "Mama!!!" He plead. "Mama! I can't breathe!" Foams of saliva dripped down the side of his mouth as he slowly lost consciousness, head on the ground.

Pierre exploded over the phone. "I'm sick of this shit!!! I'm so sick of seeing my people get murdered in this country! What the fuck!"

For some reason, however, I had a different reaction. "Pierre, I know this is really fucked up to look at, but there's something bigger going on."

"What are you talking about? Something bigger? Yea, another black man was murdered by a fuck'n cop!"

"I know, I know... But Pierre, listen to me," I begged. "You don't find the timing of this crime kind of odd? The coronavirus, and now this?"

"Are you not sympathetic to watching a fuck'n brother get murdered on live television!? Does this NOT MAKE YOU SICK TO YOUR STOMACH?" He yelled through the phone. "HOW CAN YOU NOT CARE!?"

"I DIDN'T SAY I DON'T CARE!" I shot back. "What I'm saying is that when you calm down, you might notice there's something fishy going on. I don't trust the intention behind this video being aired right now. That's all I'm saying."

"Yo! If you don't understand the pain of my people, then you're the wrong woman to be with!" He screamed. "You should've stayed with that white cop! Fuck him!"

My heart dropped after he hung up the phone.

I logged onto social media through my cell phone and started reading hundreds of people tagging independent businesses, commenting if whether or not they were a BLM supporter

– due to the motto that "If you stay silent, then you're part of the problem."

I waited a few minutes before calling Pierre again, assuming he might've needed some time to digest what he'd just seen on TV, but every time I called, it went straight to voicemail.

I then called a few of my girlfriends, to which I heard I wasn't the only one experiencing a breakup after the George Floyd incident. Apparently, couples, friends, and even business partners were falling apart during the summer of 2020, as if an invisible earthquake had ripped through the spiritual auras of communities worldwide, forcing them to quickly choose a side.

My habits began changing, such as my growing obsession with watching the news every day, which was a huge difference from the Zen meditation YouTube videos I normally watched. No longer meditating within my peaceful Brooklyn abode, turning on the news slowly became an addiction. From the moment I woke up, to the moment I lay my head to sleep, my attention was stolen by every breaking headline.

People took to the streets, marching in support of "Black Lives Matter" in all major cities across the USA. For every few who protested respectfully with picket signs held high, others resorted to violence and vandalized public properties. It was a mixture of calm and chaos, like a potent brew capable of either healing society or cursing it with its continuous chanting. Was it a time of enlightenment or a time of revenge?

I had mixed feelings about it. Part of me admired how this movement raised the collective consciousness by revealing how one person's pain is everyone's pain—the ripple effect that affects us all. Yet another part of me worried about the ramifications that some of these emotional outbursts had on innocent people who'd lost their businesses, reputations, and relationships overnight.

Yes, it was beautiful to witness how the entire world came together in solidarity to support our brothers and sisters by ensuring equality for all races and ethnicities, embracing universal love. No separation. No Hierarchy. No dominating race overruling the other. However, what was ugly to watch were the misunderstandings and fallouts that further divided families and friends, where proper communication could've healed situations instead of deepening wounds.

Amidst all this, I would occasionally call Pierre to reconnect. However, we only managed to speak once, during which he updated me about some friends of his who had been arrested for protesting. In all his stress and frustration, he preferred to connect only with people who shared his views, leaving no room for differing opinions. Eventually, he ghosted me, disappearing just as he had two years prior. History repeated itself. And just like that, the flame of our rekindled friendship was extinguished once again.

I thought of a time when Peirre and I went to the movies in Harlem to watch 2018's *"The First Purge"* filmed in the Staten Island projects. I always knew in my gut that it was our divine appointment to watch it together because of the signs and coincidences appearing across screen. Sure, it was just a Hollywood script created for *entertainment purposes only*, but like all great works of art, there are subtle messages that leave cryptic clues into dangerous truths.

It's like the Superbowl Sunday halftime show that J.Lo and Shakira put on, placing young girls inside cages to show how they're sex trafficked around the world. However, with all the dancers shaking their asses across stage underneath bright lights and fireworks, it's easy to miss the message when your attention is focused on shiny objects. Although *"The Purge,"* Rated R, does warn you of violent and gory content about a story revealing an American holiday where murder is legally permitted for 24 hours, its message can also miss the mark if one isn't open to the possibility that governments would actually pit people against each other – sometimes in the most manipulative and covert ways. Well, then, who and what do you trust? If not the movies, music, and entertainment, what in the world could be considered trustworthy if we can't even rely on love?

Living in this type of climate, I question, what is love?

All I knew was that as the world demonized police officers during the Summer of 2020, following the murder of George Floyd, it started to make more sense why my old crush, Kevin, who had been a NJ sheriff, stopped driving into NYC because of his bad gut feeling. Despite him ghosting me only three months prior to the protests, it's as if his intuition was protecting him – and he was wise to listen to it.

Unfortunately, I had gotten hurt in the process when this man who had been "potential boyfriend material" suddenly dropped off the face of the Earth. At least, things became a little clearer once I finally saw the bigger picture, but only time was able to reveal that.

Still, my heart was beginning to harden. The universe had taken away Kevin and now Pierre, for reasons beyond my control.

And what of Mike? Sure, we had closure from long ago that went beyond receiving coffee and a bagel because that entire experience had prepared me for what was to come: War.

"These aren't just shows, ya know? This is really gonna happen one day," he'd tell me whenever we'd watch an apocalyptic show. "And when it does happen, you better be prepared."

But what if war isn't just about killing others with military artillery? What if the real war is spiritual? And if it is, then what if the real enemy is unseen? And if it is unseen, then maybe it's within.

These three men I dated, Mike, Kevin, and Pierre, they weren't obligated to stay with me. Life doesn't work that way. People are free to do as they please because we each perceive life through the filter of our own lived experiences. Whether or not we agreed on the same issues, deciding to stay or to go, the real relationship was the one within.

That was the real war. And that was the real love.

Alas, as I finally started to see clearly, I decided to take a break from dating and work on loving myself a little bit more. Because one thing I was learning about life was that, as twisted as this world could be, I had a choice: I could either become a product of my own environment or rise above it. By choosing the latter, I hoped to attract an enlightened soulmate– someone I could walk side by side with in love, in truth, and in healing.

Back in Mexico, my cousin Linda invited me to an outdoor party. "We're leaving the resort to go to a real fiesta in one of these pop-up street markets."

My jaw dropped. "I'm not ready to venture out like that!"

"Jazzy! I told you I was gonna take you out of your comfort zone!"

"Why can't we eat at one of the restaurants on the strip?" I pleaded.

Linda rolled her eyes. "You did not come all the way to Mexico to stay on the same damn strip. There's a whole country to see and I'm only taking you one neighborhood away."

Shortly after, we hailed a cab and jumped in the backseat. Once outside the main tourist area, our surroundings began to change as we drove through narrow streets in nearby villages. I didn't think much of it until we stopped behind a black monster military truck blocking an intersection. Several men wearing fatigue uniforms sat above the hood, holding rifle guns pointed in the air.

"How long do we have to wait?" I asked my cousin, heart racing. She seemed unbothered and shrugged her shoulders, "I don't know. We'll move soon."

Another man-filled truck drove beside us and stopped, looking into our car window amid heavy traffic. It must've been the scariest ten minutes of my life, not knowing if they were intending to kidnap us.

Eventually, when traffic began moving again, I felt a sudden relief for continuing to head into our destination and played it cool. I didn't complain. Didn't say a word. I was just happy to finally jump out of the cab and walk into a pack-filled outdoor food market with my cousin. The two of us ready to order some tacos and drinks as we searched for an empty wooden picnic-style table to settle into.

"Time to shit-talk men," Linda declared, lifting the lid off her cerveza after sitting down.

"Ha!" I chuckled. "You really wanna kill me on this trip, don't you?" I sat across from her.

Linda giggled. "I know. Men can be difficult. Let's exchange stories."

"Who do you wanna hear about first? The younger one, the older one, the black guy, or the white guy?"

"Damn girl, you've been busy!" Linda teased.

"Well, I don't discriminate. As far as I'm concerned, they're all the same," we tapped our drinks in agreement.

Wind blew through Linda's curls. "Hey Jazzy, weren't you supposed to move to California? I could've sworn you were gonna stay out there."

I gave a devilish smirk. "I'm glad you brought that up! Because now I know exactly which guy to write about next."

She spit out some cerveza in a laugh. "You're really writing a book about the men you've dated?"

"Oh yes I am," I confessed.

"That's brave," she complimented.

I arched my eyebrows. "Brave? You were riding your bike towards a tropical storm the other day. That's brave!"

Linda giggled. "It's like my 5th time visiting Tulum, so I feel pretty comfortable. I think I might move here." With twinkling eyes, she looked at all the happy people buying tacos and burritos at the food market, dancing in their little two steps.

"Well, everything ain't always what it seems," I admitted. "I remember when I really wanted to move to California. I mean, maybe I still would, but I don't know... That honeymoon phase is over."

"What happened?" Linda asked.

"Well, it's funny how much you love riding bikes because... so did my ex. Bikes and Harleys."

Chapter 6
Na-Ma-Stay With a New Man

After the BLM protests started slowing down, I searched for something spiritually healing to maintain my peace of mind in case of any more surprises. If a worldwide outbreak killing millions of people followed by racial and political upheaval in the same calendar year wasn't enough to shock the socks off someone, I don't know what was.

Growing protective of my energy, I had delved into the ancient Japanese study of Reiki which then led me on the path to achieving my Yoga Teacher Training certificate for half the price I would've paid years ago. With so much uncertainty in the air, businesses were lowering their prices just to stay afloat while I seized the opportunity.

Every day, I opened my laptop to study online courses, learning about the intricacies of the seven chakras and how each one supports a specific function such as the heart, centering itself between the lower chakras and the higher charkas. It was considered Eastern Medicine, a compliment to Western Medicine mirroring the Yin and Yang with respect to how everything has an opposite.

A friend of mine, more of a kindred spirit who lived Midwest, noticed my personal growth and wondered why I'd yet to have a boyfriend. During covid lockdowns, we became instant friends after commenting on similar social media posts, eventually exchanging numbers and realizing we were born only two weeks apart. No coincidence there! The universe tends to bring the right people into alignment at the right time.

One day, as we were having one of our FaceTime girl-talks, she asked if I'd be willing to virtually meet one of her guy friends online.

"Girl, I don't know... The last guy I dated was Pierre and we broke up the day after my birthday. Can you believe?"

Ana-Marie sighed, eyebrows arching above her blue eyes. "Yea, I know, I'm sorry. I thought you guys were so good together. But that's why I don't want you to be alone. You did nothing wrong."

"Well, Pierre didn't feel that way. He thought I wasn't sensitive enough to Black issues and told me I should've stayed with the white cop I dated."

"It's a touchy subject," Ana-Marie admitted, pulling her long brown hair over her shoulders. "But you're not racist."

"Obviously not, but after that day, he wouldn't even give me a chance to speak."

"You know what I think?" Ana-Marie said. "Since Pierre used to go back and forth between you and his ex-girlfriend Rebecca, he probably met someone else *again* and used this as an excuse to ghost you."

"To be honest, that crossed my mind, too, because I could see if he didn't wanna speak for a few days until the dust settled, but he just completely vanished overnight."

"Yea girl, I'm not so sure about Pierre. On the other hand, I know someone else who's a little older and more mature. I'm curious to see if you two would match."

I took a deep breath. "I wish I could say I was excited, but I'm so sick of getting disappointed."

"Girl, you are so beautiful, smart, and one of the most driven people I know. Any man would be lucky to have you."

"I'm the lucky one," I emphasized. "To have a friend like you."

Hours later, she sent me his Instagram profile which pleasantly surprised me. He was a middle-aged dark-skinned man with a smooth bald head and radiant smile that drew me in with every photo of his tight-fitting muscle-tee shirt physique. *Damn, he's fine,* I thought. What sealed the deal for me, however, was that he was a Yoga Teacher! Alas, someone who was spiritually conscious. Ana-Marie might've just hit the jackpot with cupid's arrow on this one!

As I kept scrolling, I noticed he posted the book, "The Yoga Sutras of Patanjali", by Sri Swami. That meant he understood the 8 limbs of Yoga – a spiritual ladder featuring principles that when applied to our lives, supports us in living in harmonious alignment with the world. Ahimsa, which means non-violence, is the first limb setting the foundation for the rest of the climb towards enlightenment. To not cause harm to others, including yourself, is the right way to begin the journey because nothing of value comes from destroying another person, place, or even animal. Once we understand this, we move up another step, learning more ethical principles that contribute to the evolution of our consciousness that awakens to a larger truth.

If he did so much as post this book on his profile, that meant that on some level, these spiritual teachings impacted him enough to believe in them. *Yes! This could have some real potential,* I thought.

After exchanging a few Instagram DMs, I learned that he was a smart, fifty-year-old IT professional who owned a house in Northern California teaching yoga part time. Oh... My... God... Stability and spirituality!? I was impressed to find a man who blended both worlds together: locking in a professional corporate position while continuing to teach this beautiful practice of Yoga as a consciously elevated soul.

Eventually, we moved from Instagram to a six-hour Face-Time conversation, all in one day. I remember it perfectly, the first time I swiped that little green icon to answer Randal's call. He sat in front of his garage wearing a brown California inscribed Tee-shirt and a Tibetan Buddhist prayer wheel necklace hanging amid his buff chest. And his wide, straight teeth smile – it was his best feature.

"I'm a Leo," he shared.

"No wonder."

He smiled wider. "What's that mean?"

"I've never seen anyone with such a genuine smile," I replied. "You seem so sunny and optimistic. A true Leo, sign of the Lion, the sun, the king."

Randall couldn't stop smiling.

For hours, we talked. It was all going so well except for one thing: Carmen.

"You'll love Carmen. She's my ex-girlfriend but she's like a sister to me now. You'll see when you meet her." he insisted.

"Oh," I replied.

"Yea, I actually just got off the phone with her a little while ago. She was on her way out the door and I told her to put on her jacket cause it's getting a little chilly out there."

"Isn't California hot?" I assumed.

"Heck no! It snows down here in Northern California. You must be thinking of Los Angeles. Honey, California is a really big state. It's beautiful though. You'll love it."

WTF? I knew it was too good to be true, I silently thought. He's best friends with an ex? Somehow, the situation reminded me of Pierre because I too, was like a sister to him. To dig deeper, I asked a few questions: if they had kids, shared a business or were married at one point in time, to which none were true. They had absolutely no ties together other than, they were just besties.

I didn't like it because keeping an ex around could indicate unresolved issues and lingering feelings. But it's not like he had put himself on a dating app seeking companionship. How was he supposed to know someone new would walk into his life before Ana-Marie spontaneously introduced us? I decided to file it away as a mental note and continued getting to know him. After all, it was only our first conversation.

Our conversation flowed so fluidly; we didn't hang up for hours. Jokingly, he invited me to visit California to meet in person. I giggled like it was impossible to travel there so soon, but he said if I was serious about meeting, he'd make it happen.

After we said our goodbyes, he checked in every... single... day. And our connection only grew stronger with every hello. We talked about yoga, spirituality, Taoism, family, and most importantly, we talked about our future goals which naturally... aligned.

It didn't take long for him to fly me into Northern California. Maybe it was because we kept hearing about so many deaths during the pandemic, that the element of *"time"* began to take on a whole new meaning. Especially, for me, since I had just buried my grandmother from Covid, a destiny I never would've imagined. She was an 80-year-old woman living with dementia and so my entire family knew the inevitable was expected, but not like this. Not during a historical period where hundreds of thousands of people needlessly died in record-breaking numbers from the same source: A pandemic. With that, I saw each day as a gift I didn't want to waste.

And, so, there we stood. Two strangers meeting for the first time at the half-empty San Francisco airport only two weeks after speaking online. It was close to midnight. The moon glowed above Randal as he nervously handed me a dozen roses upon meeting.

"What do we do now? Do we kiss? Do we hug? I don't know," he giggled.

Seeing his smile in person made my heart melt, turning what started as an online fantasy into reality.

The drive back to his house was only 10 minutes from the airport. After parking, he jiggled his keys into the door and invited me in. "What would you like to do, miss Jasmine?" he asked.

"Hmmm... let's see." I looked around and noticed how neatly organized his earth toned house was, perfect for a Yogi. In fact, to the left was an empty meditation room adorning only a Buddha wall blanket offering sanctuary vibe's directly across opened windows, which I imagined lit the room beautifully each morning. Not a single piece of furniture filled that space, making it completely Zen. Eager to see the rest of the house, we walked toward the kitchen nuzzled next to the backyard's sliding doors. It felt peaceful, and I wanted to see more. "Well, you know I love music," I shared.

"Oh yea, you used to sing, right?" He smiled. "I have a studio upstairs."

"That's right! You told me you do!" My eyes lit up. "Show me."

Randal happily took the lead, walking up the cream-colored carpet steps towards his simplistic studio complete with three hanging guitars, keyboard, desktop computer, and profession-al microphone. Fuck! It felt like I was right where I belonged.

I took a seat by the microphone, remembering all the times I sang inside of recording booths and started humming...

Randal smiled. "You look like you're in your element."

"I am."

He took one of the guitars off the wall and started strumming its strings, sharing an original tune. "I'm still learning how to play. Bare with me."

"I love it! You're doing great."

I continued humming and then made up some words off the top of my head. Before we knew it, we were grooving.

I couldn't have felt happier. It was like I had slipped back into time, remembering why I loved music so much. Why'd I ever leave?

Was it because of my age? Was it because of money? Was it because I'd been hurt too many times and lost my inspiration? I think it was a bit of everything, but I had made peace with transitioning out of the music industry like when I applied to my humanitarian job because I couldn't make ends meet as a Dance Music Recording Artist. Despite having reached some pretty high heights, I hadn't officially "made it" as a star on the road. So eventually, I poured my energy into other areas of life and found happiness in working for a company that res-cued refugees from around the world. In all my younger years, I never would've imagined myself enjoying a nine to five, but for that particular company, I did. I was proud. The only thing missing was attracting the right partner to share my life with. Maybe it's because I knew deep down inside that I wouldn't find my other half in NY. With the world as large as it is, may-be he was somewhere else. And just maybe, tonight, he was in front of me.

Watching Randal play guitar stirred a real sense of joy within. It takes one to know one. Music was Randal's happy place, just like mine. The only difference was that he wasn't playing to earn a living because he already had a high paying corporate job. He was playing for his own personal enjoyment.

After our spontaneous jamming session, he put his guitar down and walked me across the hall, into his bedroom. When he flicked the light switch on, a star constellation sparkled across his ceiling. "You like that, right?" He smiled.

At the foot of his bed lied another alter; this one with a long white feather and some crystals. Taking a seat beside them, he explained the meaning of each one. Tourmaline for protection, Amethyst for healing and wisdom. To the right of the alter, a warm breeze blew in from the opened window. It felt peaceful.

We eventually laid in bed and pillow-talked throughout the night. Nothing erotic occurred, except for how I teased him for looking as delicious as a bar of sexual chocolate. Together we laughed until he'd ask questions about my past. What my ex-boyfriends were like, why we broke up, and what trauma I may have endured.

After a while I explained that the past was the past. I didn't care to overly discuss it because I wanted to experience a clean fresh slate. But he insisted that talking about the past was healing. I turned it back around on him.

"Why are you still friends with your ex, Carmen?" I asked.

"Oh, honey, I'd never get back with her. NEVER. But she's my friend. Sometimes people are better off that way."

"I guess, if you're co-parenting, sure. I'd agree. But if you don't have any kids or joint businesses, wouldn't that just block you from finding someone new?"

"Well, it didn't block me from finding you."

I sunk my head deeper into the pillow. "Cute answer," I replied.

"I just wanna know everything about you," said Randal. "I wanna know your past and how you came to be the person you are today."

"You're a Yogi. You out of all people should know that the present is more important than the past. I've done a lot of self-healing so talking about past lovers just doesn't resonate with me today. I prefer not to go back there."

"But you have to. If something bothers you too much to talk about, then it means you're running from it."

At that point I started to get annoyed, feeling like he was trying to play hero when I didn't need saving. Prior to that trip, I was truly enjoying my solo-time, especially after America had been protesting all Summer which eventually bled into the online dating scene. I remember reading Bumble profiles that clearly informed dating seekers to swipe left if they weren't voting for their preferred political party of interest. With so many societal transitions, I found solace when diving nose-deep into my Yoga studies instead of worrying about who my next boyfriend would be. Flipping my body over to face him, I said, "I wouldn't have taken a chance to fly all the way out here if I was too damaged for something. I just prefer not to obsess over past relationships because I already told you a few things about my ex's, and there's a lot more to me besides the men I dated. For example, I recently became a certified Yoga Teacher. Why don't we talk about that? I'm just more interested in the future. That's all."

"Yea, honey, we can talk about whatever you want to, but at some point, I'm gonna still wanna know about your past."

"What about Carmen?" I asked again. "If you're so close now, why'd you break up in the first place?"

He smirked. "That's fair. I'll tell you."

He explained that she was a recovering drug addict whom he wouldn't dream of abandoning because she had come a long way in her healing journey since their breakup, and that ten years of friendship was something he would never be willing to give up. That's when I understood their bond was deeper than I thought.

I could relate.

Not only was my ex, Mike, an alcoholic, but I even had an ex-fiancé before meeting Mike whom I had buried over a decade ago. I hadn't mentioned him in this book until now. Cocaine is a hell of a drug.

In fact, coming from the world of dance music, I'm surprised I never got hooked on it myself. For years, I witnessed DJ's sniffing coke by their turntables or spilling white particles into little plastic bags by the bar. It wasn't a secret that coke was easily available in the nightlife scene. Club owners did it, beautiful women did it, and even bouncers patting down people at the door did it. But then of course, there were always people like me who never needed an extra "kick" because drugs weren't our thing.

But when you love someone, you don't want to see them die – even though the fate of their choices may not be up to you. And when they leave, it's not because they wanted to, it's because drugs killed them.

After Randal explained everything about Carmen, I sympathized because I knew if my ex-fiancé were still alive, we would've remained friends too. However, the truth was, I didn't like it. Maybe I just wanted him to be free from the past despite her transitioning from lover to friend.

The next morning, three of the loudest doorbells startled me out of bed.

WTF? I instantly sat up.

Randal, unbothered, slowly cracked his eyes open. "Oh, those are just my cleaning ladies."

"Excuse me," I giggled. "You pay people to clean your house?"

"The things that money can buy," Randal joked, wind blowing through the windows.

My excitement grew as I walked over to the window to catch a better view of the neighborhood.

He lived on a hill, like San Francisco streets overlooking parks and nature trails. Off into the distance, a hawk soared amid a clear blue sky; these suburbs offering an open space of peace and tranquility. Was this real? For a moment, I felt sorry for myself for having lived in NYC all these years. What the hell had I been missing?

Randal came from behind and wrapped his arms around my waste.

"Is it ok that I hold you like this?" he asked.

We'd already broken the ice by sleeping in the same bed, but we were trying to take things slow – all things considering.

Since my roundtrip ticket was only booked for 5 days, he wanted to show me around town as much as possible. That's when I learned how much he loved riding bikes, which to my surprise, I found therapeutic too. We packed a few things to hit the road with, including one of his favorite books, "The Taoist Way," and rode off into one of the nearby nature trails on our first day. After passing a duck-filled lake, we'd find a patch of grass to lay our blankets on, and rest. It was heavenly. Literally. Heavenly.

Now don't get me wrong, I've traveled to plenty of suburbs on the East Coast, visiting beautiful places deep in Long Island, New Jersey, Connecticut, Virginia, Washington DC, and Florida. I even vacationed near Canada's forest resorts like "Lake George" and made it across the West Coast visiting gorgeous desert land in Arizona and Nevada. But something about Northern California felt majestic. It was the perfect blend of modern-day living mixed with nature's healing abyss – something that urban cities lacked, like the concrete jungle of NYC.

Out here I could breathe. I could think. I could relax.

For the next few days, Randal drove us to different parks with a pair of bicycles in the back. He was obviously a nature boy, always dressed casually wearing earth toned colored T-shirts, light fatigue pants, and mountain boots or sneakers. With two bicycles handy, we were always prepared to ride through a scenic nature trail. I never knew where we'd end up, but I always knew it would be good. One day, as we sat amid the floor bark of some of the forests tallest redwood trees, we talked about the inevitable: The end of the world.

"You know, my family's from Louisianna. They're not from Cali," Randal admitted.

"Oh... Wow. That's interesting."

"Yea, my dad moved my mom out to California when he got the job offer, so we were the first in our family to move out West. All their brothers and sisters stayed behind."

"I guess sometimes, it's worth making that major life change."

He took a protein bar out from his bag and took a bite. "Yeah, it seemed to work out for them cause we're still here, but every now and then, we'd go back to visit. That's where I learned to shoot."

Now I was intrigued. "Tell me more."

He offered a piece of his bar. "You wanna bite?"

"No, I want you to tell me more about how you learned to shoot."

He giggled. "Yea, well, in Louisianna it's different. Me and all my cousins, aunts, and uncles would shoot for fun. We'd hunt rabbits and farm animals. My uncle was real good. He'd shoot gators. I couldn't fuck with that. My point is, it's good to know how to use guns because you can protect yourself, your family, and your property."

"Wait, wait, wait... Mr. Yogi," I sarcastically joked. "You know about the Yamas and the Niyamas, Ahimsa, being the first limb of Yoga which means non-violence. So, I'm surprised. Are you saying you like hunting and killing?"

"No, no, no," Randal laughed. "Not at all. That's not what I'm saying. What I am saying is that if shit were to really go down, worse than this little pandemic that everyone's so afraid of, people are gonna need to know how to protect themselves."

"I knew someone else who used to talk like that," I admitted, thinking about my conspiracy theorist ex-boyfriend, Mike.

"Think about it. You can't let them take away our second amendment. You know, my mother asked if I was gonna vote for Biden. I told her I would, as long as they don't take away our right to bear arms."

"So, you're saying you would vote for Trump?" I asked.

"I'm saying I won't, but I would... cause I'm not giving up my guns," he said.

"And you're a Black man," I stated the obvious. "Just as I thought. Not everything's about race."

"Oh honey, who people vote for shouldn't be a black or white thing. I'm so beyond that bullshit."

"I'll admit, I don't know much about politics. Actually, to be fair, I heard the Democratic party doesn't wanna completely abolish guns. They just wanna make it stricter to get them. Aside from guns, I will admit, I like you're *frame of mind* because at least you're not voting out of peer pressure."

"Fuck peer pressure," Randal said, sounding like a true Leo. "I've never seen this country so divided in my entire life. But since I'm not a politician to know all the secret intricacies that go on in the white house, I really don't care. That's why I come out into nature – to get away from all the bullshit."

"And yet just another reason why I like you. Now, grab me another protein bar from your bag."

"Kiss me first," Randal leaned into me and interlaced his dark-skinned fingers into my caramel toned ones. Maybe that Indian proverb that says *a man's highest calling is to protect a woman*, was about to be put to the test.

"Hey quick question... Have you ever camped so far out in the wilderness, that you came across a bear or wild animal?"

Randal arched his eyebrows, "Honey, I've seen a lot of shit in these woods. And none of it scares me – as long as I'm prepared."

Chapter 7
Diamond Rings and Karmic Soul Ties

"Don't talk about Trump," Linda challenged. "I hate that man."

"I didn't say I love him, but I can't say I hate him either," I replied.

"Please don't tell me you're a Trumper."

"I'm an Independent. I don't associate one hundred percent with either party."

Linda rolled her eyes, taking another sip from her cerveza.

"I'm actually a fan of Marianne Williamson," I continued.

"Who's that?"

"Oh my God. Girl! I love her! She's probably not the toughest candidate, but in my opinion, she's the smartest. She started as a self-help author before running for President, but then dropped out of the race."

"So, what's the obsession?" My cousin seemed curious.

"It's just the way she spoke. As a self-help guru of sorts, she was able to reach people in both parties-- Republicans and

Democrats. But there's a lot of shady shit that goes on behind the scenes. I guess that's why it's good to travel sometimes... to get away from all that."

It was already 9PM, sun was down, and the salsa band got louder.

"Hey, don't they play house-music in Tulum?" I asked.

"Jazzy, there's a million clubs out here, but you're too chicken shit to go anywhere. You think the Cartels are gonna get you or something."

"I mean... I'm not *that* paranoid, but it is my first time here and as women, shouldn't we be careful of sex trafficking? Maybe for men, it's different but we're vulnerable."

"Oh girl, please. Speak for yourself. If you keep thinking that way, you're never gonna enjoy your trip. As for me, after watching this little salsa band, I'm gonna hit a real club. You're welcome to come but if not, I'll go alone and make some new friends."

Looking around, I saw large palm tree leaves blowing in the wind amid hanging outdoor lights and felt uneasy, like I had to be careful of my surroundings. I just didn't know why?

Linda and I shared a cab driving back to the strip. Only, our driver decided to take country backroads. I silently panicked as we zoomed passed cars on a narrow dirt road amid rocks and pebbles – without streetlights in utter darkness.

Sitting beside me, Linda shared pictures of her mermaid friend in Tulum while my nerves jittered under my skin. Why was Linda making it obvious that we were American tourists, talking loudly enough that this stranger could hear our conversation driving us in the middle of nowhere? If the cabdriver wanted to, he'd drive off toward an unknown location. Heart racing, I wanted to make it back to my glamping tent as fast as possible.

Once we approached my glamping destination, I leaped out of the cab and ran into my room. Linda did exactly what she said she was going to do and borrowed a flashlight from a hotel security guard in search of nearby nightclubs on foot. I thought she was fearless; walking alone where only the moonlight's glow amid distant stars replaced streetlights. One thing I learned quickly about Tulum was that they really kept their jungle-life environment authentic, despite it becoming one of the best-kept party towns in the world. But being a true New Yorker, I wouldn't let my guard down that easily.

Back in my room, I decided to do exactly what I said I was going to do, opening my laptop to type about my journey into the California mountains with Randal because after all, this was my solo writer's retreat – and writing words across the page is where I felt safest.

Fluffing two pillows behind my neck for support, I sat up in bed and caught a few glimpses of the wooden elephant Ganesha centerpiece amid the coffee table in the middle of the room. Its symbol of protection along with cricket sounds outside my window soothed me, and I'm sure there was a toad leaping somewhere nearby the bed. All of it was enough for me to appreciate this foreign environment and do what I came here to do – continue writing my story.

After having spent five days with Randal, I returned to NY with a newfound appreciation for nature along with my hope for a solid relationship. Randal indeed seemed more promising than the other men I'd dated: Mike, Pierre, and Kevin. But it was still too early in the honeymoon stages to cement it. Every day we FaceTimed until Randal booked me a returning flight to stay for a lengthy three-weeks.

On my first day back, Randal drove us up a hill toward the Land of Medicine, a redwood refuge Buddhist retreat tucked away in the heart of the Santa Cruz mountains. Outside its gates, I could see leaves bustling in the winds amid multicolored Tibetan flags hanging from tree to tree. Each one, rectangular shaped, offering printed prayers within its fabric. Of course, I couldn't read them because they were too far from view, but Randal explained their meaning and said I would've loved this place if it were open. Too bad, the gates were locked during the pandemic.

"Can you see from here?" Randal pointed outside his car window. "Look through the bars and read the sign." It read, LAND OF MEDICINE: *A Center for Healing and Developing a Good Heart*. He drove around, wanting to show me as much as possible, but it was a ghost town.

"You see, this is what I mean about the pandemic," Randal said. "Who's gonna get sick walking around these woods? Neither of us are wearing masks and we're both fine, breathing fresh air. They got everybody shook for nothing."

"Well, at least you tried. And at least now I know this place exists. Thank you for showing me," I said.

"You're welcome, honey. I just know you would've loved this place, you being a new Yoga Teacher and all," he winked, and then turned the steering wheel, headed for the next place.

"You like shopping?" He asked.

"Of course. I'm a woman," I giggled.

"I bet you like diamonds, too." He smirked. "Black diamonds."

I blushed. In one of our FaceTime conversations, I had told him I preferred a black diamond engagement ring over the traditional clear ones. Not many women desired this, but I always wanted something different. Though I had to admit, taking me to view engagement rings this early in our relationship wrecked my nerves.

When we got to the mall, he took me inside a jewelry store to check my ring size. I didn't know whether to feel excited or scared. In less than a few weeks, I was turning 40. Was this really happening? It's not like he was proposing, but the mere fact that he was even thinking about it to the point of taking aligned action meant that he was serious about manifesting it. I slid my finger through the ring size measurer, changing rounds until finding the perfect fit. I couldn't help but think that my dreams of finding my person were actually happening by 40 because I had written it years ago. In my old journal, I affirmed, *I will spend my 40ᵗʰ birthday with my husband.* Yet still, when looking down at my ring finger, I questioned if this was too soon because we hadn't even reached six months of dating yet, and there was still so much to learn about each other.

Back up the Santa Cruz mountains we drove, cruising on curvy cliffs offering scenic views. Eventually we drove into one of the parking lots and leaped out of the car to venture into the woods without bikes. Hiking down an easy trail, we stopped by a tree log to rest our feet.

"I wonder how Carmen's doing? I should give her a call," he said. "I really want you to meet her on this trip."

"Can I ask you something?"

"What's up?" Randal asked, standing in front of the tree log I sat on.

I looked up. "Do you still have feelings for her?"

Randal turned and stomped off, huffing and puffing. I felt confused. What just happened? Why did my question send him away? I waited to see how far he'd walk before turning around.

He looked back. "How can you ask me that after I just took you window shopping for engagement rings?"

Jaw dropping, I was stunned at how angry he'd become.

"It's just a question," I said. "A question that came up *because* we're on the topic of engagement rings, and since you've been talking about Carmen since the first day we met, it makes me wonder if there's still something deeper... something that maybe you're even hiding from yourself."

Randal looked stunned. "I can't believe that's what you're thinking about when I've been showing you how much I care. Haven't I been proving to you how serious I am about us?"

"Yes, but that's not the p –

Randal walked off again. This time further away as I stubbornly stayed on that tree log, refusing to run after him. I knew I didn't know my way around these woods and that I had no way of getting back because he was the one with the car. But I wanted to see how far he'd go before turning back. I sat there, cool, calm, and collected thinking, *I've seen this all before. A man comes in all hot 'n heavy until BOOM! They switch up. Day turns into night, and good turns into bad.*

A few minutes later, Randal and I looked for each other at the same time – as if we were both testing each other. He wanted to see if I'd run after him. I wanted to see if he'd come back. We met in the middle and then walked to the car together.

The ride back was tense. Neither Randal nor I spoke much. Staring outside the passenger window, I looked at all the happy couples eating outdoors amid fancy restaurants and thought how everything was just a dream. Had I been that naïve to think that nothing was without its challenges? I just didn't know if this was our first fight or a red flag? Eventually, Randal spoke. Although I can't remember exactly what he said, whatever it was, it was enough for me to pop.

"Oh my god! I'm so sick of this shit! Why do men always do this!? Fuck! I don't even care anymore!" I yelled.

Randal arched his eyebrows. "Oh, hell no! Wow! So, this is the real you? That's why I wanted to talk about your past because you just said *why do men always do this shit.* So, now I gotta pay for what every man did to you before?"

"No!" I shot back. "You don't have to pay for anything because I wasn't even looking for a man when we met. I was fine being single! I was working on myself, and I was happy. In fact, I was so happy that I didn't want to obsess over ex's because I was ready for a fresh clean slate. But you're the one who blew up because of a SIMPLE QUESTION ABOUT YOUR EX!"

"Fine, Jasmine! All men are shit! Be alone if that's what you want! Forget I showed you rings today!"

I took a deep breath, inhaled and exhaled and then silently thought to myself, *I am way too smart to let someone mindfuck me into thinking that I'm the one with the problem, when he's the one who was triggered over a simple question about his ex – on the day we looked at engagement rings, nonetheless.*

I couldn't wait to get back to the house so I could jump out of the car and blow off some steam. Whether it was just our first fight that we could work through or a red flag that meant we had to part ways, I needed some space. Different situations call for different types of space.

It was getting closer to the end of my Tulum trip with only two days remaining. Linda and I were leaving on separate days and decided to see each other one last time. After having some girl-talk inside a hotel pool, we learned more about each other than we ever did back home. Something about two middle aged women sharing stories underneath a Buddha-themed swimming pool in the tropics felt spiritually therapeutic, to say the least.

"You seem pretty serious about this move to Mexico," I said.

"I sure am," said Linda. "You can't tell me you don't love this place, too?"

"Oh, I can see why you love it. Believe me. You know what? You got one to life to live. Try it out. If it works out, it works out. If it doesn't, it doesn't. But at least you'll know." I held my nose and sunk my head underwater, then came back up for air.

Linda did the same, dipping into the water one last time before jumping out of the pool to dry herself off with a towel. Sun shining brightly, it didn't take much for her bikini line tan to show off her arms. It was proof of a good time. And besides the fact that we didn't dance the night away at one of these nightclubs, at least we got the chance to share girl-secrets that would forever remain between her and I – along with our photos on a rainy day beneath a heart themed waterfall.

After Linda left, another middle-aged woman jumped in the pool, but she was older. I was 41; she was 53. We made small talk, continuing the conversation about love and relationships that started from our tattoos – mine's a delicate dove, and hers, the peaceful om symbol. She explained how she got her tattoo during the year of her separation, right before her divorce. She said that despite having three beautiful children, releasing her ex-husband was the best decision she ever made for her peace of mind. I wasn't against marriage. Not at all. But the truth was that I'd heard more stories told from the lips of divorce's than I did from happy couples. And that spoke volumes.

Before heading back to our rooms, she invited me to join some friends for a shamanic Temazcal ceremony; a fire ritual held inside of a sweat lodge where people gathered amidst herbs and stones. She explained how its purpose was to purify participants, welcoming their renewal as they rid themselves of past toxicity and emotional baggage.

I always knew that heat was known for opening pores. Steam rooms and saunas detoxify people, so there's no doubt that a fire ceremony could do the same. But the idea of sitting too closely to people within a small space you weren't allowed to leave, didn't feel too good. I wasn't even sure of my own capability, if I could suffocate easily or if someone else could. So, I passed on it. Linda's voice rang in my mind. *If you keep being afraid, you're not gonna enjoy your trip.* I still felt like it was the right thing to do, and in a different setting, I'm sure I'd try it.

Back in my room, I removed my wet sticky bathing suit from my body and took a hot shower enclosed by uniquely shaped bamboo sticks. I'm sure anyone could've given themselves a peep show, but that was the beauty of being in the jungle. After drying myself off, I went back to my usual routine and opened my laptop. Only, I have to admit, as much as I loved the healing qualities of nature, I started to miss the security of NYC because out here, anyone could walk into one of these hotels or glamping tents and take whatever and *whoever* they wanted; even a safety lock box was light enough to carry out and steal. I couldn't help thinking worst case scenario. Maybe because I'm a New Yorker. I've seen too much.

"Guess what I ordered?" Randal asked, from the sofa.

"What?"

"Cheesecake."

I smiled from ear to ear. "Awww... Thank you!" I walked over to hug him and then pulled out the cheesecake from the brown paper bag.

Randal smiled back. "I remember you saying it was your favorite dessert."

"You wanna share?" I offered, cutting a piece.

"No babe, you enjoy it..."

"Well, I learned today that you have a bit of a temper."

"Yea, you got one, too," he said.

"You know I'm not gonna silently agree with everything you say, right?" I then took my first bite. "Ummm... this is delicious."

"You probably should... I'm joking," he laughed.

"You better be," I winked. "You know, window-shopping for rings today really made me think. Maybe it's too soon to look into that."

"Honey, I'm not trying to marry you right now. I just figured if you're gonna make a move all the way to California, then you're gonna want some guarantees. So, I was just showing you that my mind is on the future."

"I appreciate that," I said, still wanting to discuss Carmen, but I left it alone.

The next day, Randal drove us to the beach. Immediately after removing our footwear to walk along the sand, he received a call from Carmen crying. He answered quickly. "What happened?" He asked, and then walked off to speak to her privately.

When he came back, he explained how she was crying over last night's date who made her feel slutty for how she dressed. She told Randal that she took her time doing her make-up and hair to look really attractive for someone who insulted her the moment they sat down for dinner. Crying uncontrollably, she vented about possibly remaining single forever. Randal fumed, angry over how men kept taking advantage of her.

I was confused. Were his feelings for her strictly platonic or were they deeper? As we walked barefoot closer to the water, I stopped and looked out into the vast sea.

"Are you okay?" Randal asked.

I held back my tears. "Yea. Everything's fine. I'm just looking at the ocean because I don't get to see this back in NY with all those brick buildings."

"Okay... I'm gonna go for a run, but I'll jog slowly so you can catch up," he kissed my cheek and started on his way.

I looked down towards my feet, digging my toes into the wet sand and felt my intuition buzzing. Something about Randal and Carmen's relationship didn't feel right. Why was she calling him crying when she knew I was here from out-of-town? And why did Randal give her such easy access almost every day? Not to mention, the way he ran off after hanging up the phone with her which gave him less energy to bond with me because he had already bonded with her over the phone. I just wondered if he was aware of it.

I eventually snapped out of my thoughts and joined Randal's jogging. But holding my feelings inside felt suffocating, like I was repressing my true emotions. Randal must've felt that my energy was off because we came to a full stop. He then bent over and rolled up the bottom of his pants to prevent too much water from splashing over them.

"You sure you alright?" He asked.

"Yes... It's beautiful out here."

From where we stood, all you could see was an empty clean beach and a couple of seagulls. I decided to enjoy the fact that the sea-salt ocean breeze warmed my skin on that Spring California day during the pandemic. Whether it would last or not, I appreciated the present moment for what it was because, things change.

Back at his house, my cell phone would ring from friends and family checking in on me; everyone curious to see how this long-distance romance was unfolding. *Are you gonna move out there?* They'd ask. Especially, Ana-Marie who called the most because she was the one who introduced us.

"Relationships can be hard, but I know this can work. Don't give up too soon," she told me.

We'd been talking over the phone as I walked up and down Randal's block, greeting a hummingbird that flew by. I was definitely in another world.

"I know, but he's besties with his ex-girlfriend. The thought of leaving everyone behind to move into his territory and then accept the fact that he has a decade-long history with a clingy ex-girlfriend doesn't sound too thrilling," I complained, despite my sunny picturesque surroundings.

"Well, have you met her yet?"

"No... I think it's too soon."

"I think you should meet her and get it over with."

"Yea, but I think in these beginning stages of dating it should be about *me and him* connecting. Not introducing his third-party ex-girlfriend-turned-bestie."

"Girl, I agree with you. Trust me. I wouldn't like it either, but I just think if he's that bonded to her than you have no choice but to see what it's all about."

I sighed. "Unfortunately... you might be right. Somehow, this isn't how I imagined things."

I then told Ana-Marie that Randal and I went window-shopping for engagement rings and she screeched in excitement.

"Girl! Shut up! Oh my god! I'm gonna be one of your maids of honors! Imagine a California wedding outdoors surrounded by nature and all your friends and family. You'll have to fly them in! Oh my god! A destination wedding! I'm so excited for you!"

"No! I'm not even thinking about that yet. I mean, yea! It sounds beautiful and of course I want that, but I don't wanna get ahead of myself yet."

"I know, it's scary," Ana-Marie said. "Nothing's guaranteed. But I know you can manifest this."

I thought about what I had previously written in my journal about spending my 40th birthday with my husband and realized that my manifestations were coming true. So, why was I pushing this away?

After hanging up, I spoke with other friends and family who were also eager for me to commit. My mother even congratulated me for *finally* finding a man and invited him to NY for a family dinner the following week.

"We're gonna pop the champagne bottle cause Jasy's gotta new man!" She joked over the phone. I felt a bit confused, unsure if this was a good thing or a bad thing that my family and friends were so desperate for me to settle down. Why so soon, anyway? It felt like life or death.

"Ask him. Just ask him if he'll fly into NY for a big family dinner," my mother asked over the phone.

"Mom, it's way too soon."

"No, it's not. Just ask. If he says, no, then he won't come. Just ask."

I really wasn't ready for Randal to see my apartment or to spend that much time together back-to-back because our three-week trip was already a lot. But after inviting Randal to NY, he jumped on the opportunity with a clear and resounding YES! I was shocked. Without hesitation, he bought a round-trip ticket to JFK right in front of my eyes.

Chapter 8
When Secrets Spill, Who's Gonna Clean It Up? God?

Out of all the people Randal met, my Italian stepfather's brother, Salvator, shaking his left leg in an Elvis Presley impersonation singing, "I'm All Shook Up," around the pasta-filled dinner table is what entertained him the most. He couldn't stop laughing at how much fun he had, comparing that part of the family to a real-life Soprano's episode.

Everyone got along. My siblings, my aunts and uncles, my mother and stepfather – they all approved of Randal and thought for sure I'd be moving to California as we each toasted with our wine glasses in hand. Both, Randal and I, felt good about our decision to spend time in NY together even though it was all happening so fast. I wrote off our argument over his ex-girlfriend Carmen and didn't bother bringing it up again. Until... I saw a text from her appear across his phone.

She asked him how his time in NY was going.

I arched my eyebrows, looking at Randal, "Why can't she *wait* until you get back to California to ask? You don't think it's kind of intrusive to contact you while you're out-of-town with me?"

Randal accused me of being jealous and told me I had to meet her next because he had made the effort to fly in and meet my family.

"Randal... Carmen is not your mother, your father, or your sister. She's your ex-girlfriend."

"She's my friend!" He irritated. "And if you try to make me choose between you or my friends, you're gonna lose!"

I cocked my head to the side, feeling slightly disrespected. I never told him to cut her off. In fact, I had sympathized with their friendship because it reminded me of the connection I shared with my ex-fiancé whom I buried years ago from hard drugs. But from what I was learning about Carmen is that she'd been clean the past couple of years and no longer needed help, which led me to believe her reason for holding on was just in case she could rekindle their flame.

"Fine. I'll meet her!" I told Randal. "But I never said I wouldn't! All I was trying to say was that an ex-girlfriend shouldn't be prioritized over a new girlfriend if she's supposably you're past."

God, I've been here before. I thought. *Pierre.*

There were a few differences, of course. I remember when Pierre and I had pillow-talk after recording, "North Star," in his uptown Harlem apartment. Surrounded by flickering tealights and smooth playing music, Pierre, admitted to being confused between Rebecca and me. The next day, he even went so far as to say he thought he was in love with the both of us, confessing right before I ran down the steps, disappearing into the subway because he didn't choose me – not on that day anyway.

I took Randal sight-seeing around Williamsburg Brooklyn and other trendy neighborhoods where my friends joined us for dinner and drinks at live music venues. Despite enjoying ourselves, sometimes I'd wonder if I should keep my guard up or let it down. Whenever he'd put his arms around me, I'd feel comfortable leaning in, but then my mind would tell me not to get too deep because if it didn't work out, I'd fall apart. We were becoming too close too soon.

How many times can someone fall in love, and still call it *real love*? Of course, each person is unique. But how often can you switch partners, your heart beating and breaking for each of them? Maybe I wasn't ready for this? Maybe I didn't trust it? Maybe the speed of our relationship was developing too fast? I didn't realize the pace would take off the way that it did. And, what really made it heavy for me were the early talks about marriage, the expectations from family and friends, and a lingering ex-girlfriend that I wasn't too comfortable with. I needed air.

We were on the verge of breaking up when my mother told me over the phone, "I don't want your 40th birthday to be ruined over this. It's next week. If he talks to you about his ex-girlfriend, don't start any drama. Eventually, that girl will fade away."

"Why is it so important that I make this relationship work?" I asked.

"Because I want you to be happy," she said. "Isn't this what you wanted?"

"Of course. But there should be a natural process to this. Instead, it feels like everyone's breathing down my neck like this is my last opportunity on Earth! Is it because of my age?" I asked.

"Look, I would never want you to do something you're un-sure of. But you can't let his ex-girlfriend intimidate you into leaving just because they share history. You're gonna have to give her a little competition. And remember, he's your boy-friend right now. Not hers."

I took a deep breath. "All this pressure is sucking the air out of me. Now, I have to fight for him? We just met! If I was 21 years old, would anyone even be up my ass about this? And what about him? No one's forcing him to make this work and he's TEN YEARS OLDER! I guess it's because he's a MAN."

"I know it's not fair, but men play by a different set of rules."

"Yea, well, I gotta go. Thanks for talking."

"I love you," my mom said. "Call me if you need me."

The truth was, I didn't want to break up with Randal but the more pressure I felt, the less I was able to fall in love. My emotions felt blocked because there were these invisible shoes I needed to fill – like some predetermined path I was expected to walk as a woman. I was a childless 39-year-old woman turn-ing 40 in one week and everything around me pointed to mar-riage as if it were the ultimate goal. Before meeting Randal, I imagined myself going to Hawaii alone to celebrate my mile-stone in the ocean. It was supposed to be a self-healing trip, a chance to immerse myself in the water as a symbol of renewal. Instead, I somehow got caught up in a whirlwind romance that took me by surprise. It was beautiful, romantic, fun, and chal-lenging, but it simply wasn't what I had originally planned.

Before leaving NY, Randal removed his sterling silver prayer-wheel necklace and put it around my neck.

"I want you to have this," Randal offered.

He really was a nice guy. Not perfect, but who was? He came close enough to it, other than the fact that he was a little too close for comfort with Carmen, but maybe my mother was right. Maybe I shouldn't complain about it.

A week later, Randal FaceTimed to wish me a Happy 40th Birthday and then flew me into San Francisco, making plans to celebrate my milestone at a romantic restaurant followed by a weekend-long trip of camping underneath the stars, but first, he wanted me to meet Carmen.

Everything sounded so nice – he was going to bring his acoustic guitar, a few Taoist books, snacks and wine. I was excited about all of the above, just not the part about meeting Carmen. But I thought, *maybe when I meet her in person, it won't be so bad.*

The day came when I finally met Carmen in his house. I'd been playing some soulful house music at a low volume in the kitchen when she agreed to meet me over the phone.

"Hi," she smiled as she walked through the door. "Oh, this is different. You never listen to house music, Randal. Usually, it's peaceful meditation."

Already she was criticizing, I thought.

We were both brunette Latinas the same height and weight, in a similar age range with her only three years older. She wore an oversized white sweater, black spandex and sneakers.

Standing by the kitchen aisle, she asked Randal, "Hey honey, can you get me a glass of water. It's really hot out there."

He poured her some tap water from the kitchen faucet. "Hey, you know what? I'm gonna run to the store and buy a bunch of bottled water while you girls get a chance to talk," he said. "Alone."

"What?" Carmen looked worried. Quickly, she threw her car keys across the room. "Take my car instead of yours! So, you don't have to go into the garage."

Randal caught her keys in midair. "Oh, thanks Carmen."

Already, we were off to a bad start. I felt that she was trying to piss all over her territory when she threw her car keys at him, offering the comfort of her car in front of me. In fact, it infuriated me.

After he shut the door behind him, Carmen and I took a seat at the kitchen table, sitting right across from each other.

Rolling up her sleeves, she cut right to the chase. "Look. You don't have to worry about me. I'm his ex-girlfriend, but we're just friends. The truth is, I fucked up years ago and I know he'll never take me back. We've just grown to become the best of friends, but we are over and done with."

I smiled sweetly, "I appreciate you being upfront, but can I be honest?"

"Sure," she said, placing her elbow on the table as she held her chin up with one hand to listen.

"I don't know how much Randal told you about me, but I'm a very spiritual person just like he is, which is part of the reason we get along... You know this about him. So, I'm pretty sure without a shadow of a doubt, that you're a beautiful person, but the issue I have is that I think it's a conflict of interest for Randal to have two women around him who might possibly, both, be in love with him."

She released her hand from her chin and fell back into her chair, "He's gonna learn a lot from you."

I continued, "I'm not suggesting you would do something with him behind my back because I don't know you. What I am saying is... I'm sure you still love him... *in that way*. Am I right?"

She smirked, "You're not a stupid bitch."

I cocked my head sideways, thinking, Was that a backhanded compliment? *There is no way in hell I'm going to have this woman in my life.* It wasn't because of judgement. It was about discernment.

I know my mother told me not to let Randal's ex-girlfriend intimidate me into leaving, but as far as I was concerned, Carmen should've been a closed door. I don't see how holding onto an ex was healthy for a new relationship, other than the fact that Randal wasn't looking for me when he found me. We were spontaneously introduced.

I heard Ana-Marie's voice in my head. *"Relationships can be hard, but I know this can work. Don't give up too soon,"* my friend had told me. But despite all the advice I received about making our relationship work, I couldn't picture myself moving to California where Randal was my only support system and Carmen was his bestie.

Randal eventually came back with water bottles as Carmen raised herself up from the kitchen table getting ready to leave. She leaned in to hug me. "Maybe one day we can all go to New York together!" She suggested, wrapping her arms around me.

I was done.

Inviting herself to come to NY after indirectly admitting she still loved him on the first day we met – was over the top. What made her think I'd want all of us to take vacations together? After she left, Randal asked me what I thought of her.

Sarcastically, I told him the truth. "I think she's still in love with you. Some friend."

Later that evening when I stepped into the shower, I stood there naked in body and soul, and bowed my head underneath cascading water, interlacing my fingers to pray.

God, I need to talk to you.

I know I prayed for a husband on my 40th birthday. I know I prayed about moving into a big house, specifically out West.

California or Arizona... Somewhere hot and sunny. So, God... if you're listening... I see that everything Randal's offering is part of my answered prayer, so, why won't I accept this blessing?

I'm so afraid of making a mistake that I don't wanna leave him, but the truth is I don't wanna be in this situation. Should I fight to keep him, or should I walk away? And, if I walk away, does that mean I gave up too soon and that I can't persuade things to go my way? Why am I struggling to make a decision?

Choices. It should be easy to make them, but for some reason, it's not for me.

And God, I know no one's perfect. I'm willing to go through ups and downs with Randal but not if there's another woman involved. Even if he's not cheating because she's a "friend," it still feels like emotional cheating. So, can you help? If he's meant to be mine, can you work things out for us? But, if he's that stubborn about keeping Carmen in his life, can you separate us? I just don't wanna be in a third-party situation. I want something healthy and vibrant, free from the past.

I turned the shower knob off and then grabbed the wall towel, drying my body amid the steam cloud hitting my skin. Something about praying made me feel as light as a feather. I then wrapped the towel around my body and walked over to the sink to brush my teeth. Looking up at Randal's mirror affirmation, it read: *Trust the Process.* Every morning and night we'd see that same message, but this occasion felt different.

After changing into some loose-fitting pajamas, I crawled into bed next to Randal and fell asleep peacefully, knowing that I'd sent my prayers up to God.

The next morning, I walked downstairs into the living room and turned on the TV in search of Tai-Chi and Reiki YouTube videos. Since our relationship was becoming rocky, I thought watching some spiritual content together would be good for the soul. For about an hour, we flipped through YouTube lessons taught by spiritual Gurus teaching the history of Tai Chi,

Reiki, Taoism, and other spiritual modalities. Randal seemed to enjoy them while eating breakfast but eventually went back upstairs to play guitar.

A few minutes later, I followed him inside the studio to ask if he was ok. I don't remember word-for-word what we said, but I remember him feeling so frustrated that he stormed outside of the house. I remember it having something to do with me not being pleased enough... Again, I was shocked. I knew he wanted to ride bikes that day, but I wasn't particularly in the mood especially after having had that face-to-face sit down with his ex-girlfriend the day before. In my mind, staying indoors to watch spiritual videos was helping me shift my mood to something more positive. And no – I wasn't thinking about what Randal wanted at that moment because the thought of relocating to California was beginning to bother me.

Randal stormed back inside the house and asked why I wasn't happy? I told him I was fine, but I just felt like staying indoors to watch spiritual content, assuming he would've enjoyed it too since we always connected on spirituality. But he didn't believe me. The two of us stood, face to face, in front of his living room TV. He shook his head, "No, you're not happy here. No matter what I do for you, you're not happy."

I didn't know what to do. He placed both of his hands on his hips and looked like he was about to explode. "You should leave," he said.

"What!?" I responded.

"You need to go. Now. If you're not happy here, just leave," he demanded.

"Where am I gonna go? I don't live in California."

"I don't care! Just go!" He yelled. He grabbed my arm and pulled me towards his door. "Just get out!"

"I will!" I responded. "But it doesn't have to be like this! Just give me a second!"

Tears streaming down my face, I ran upstairs to his bedroom and started packing my bags. As I stuffed each item into my suitcase, I cried in confusion, wondering why he exploded so quickly. But then again, I had prayed the night before, asking God to help me make the decision because I couldn't do it myself. If we were meant to be, then God would've worked things out for us. But if Randal would remain stubborn about keeping Carmen close, then I'd rather not be in a third-party situation.

After walking down the stairs with my suitcase in hand, I passed Randal with crying eyes, opened the door and left.

Down the sunny street I walked in emotional disarray. What the fuck just happened? I didn't know where I'd go, but a part of me was relieved to get away because the energy turned toxic. Immediately, my phone rang... It was Carmen.

"Oh my God! Jasmine. Are you okay? Randal just told me he kicked you out," Carmen said.

"Carmen!" I yelled into the phone. "He called YOU after he kicked ME out!? That says EVERYTHING!"

"I just wanted to know if you were ok because I can come get you!"

"Thank you, but no thank you! I'll figure it out!" I hung up on her.

Afterwards, I called one of my girlfriends to vent. She helped me find a nearby hotel through Google search and advised me to stay there overnight and then take a flight back to NY in the morning. Randal eventually called, asking me if I was safe and if I needed money to get around. "Money!?" I yelled into the phone. "Keep it!"

He tried to offer some help, sounding as if he had felt bad for exploding the day before. I don't know what triggered his outburst, but the one thing I understood was how much he tried to make the relationship work. He constantly flew me out to California and even made the effort to meet my family. I couldn't say he wasn't serious. Whether I'm right or wrong, I just kept feeling that one of our major challenges – aside from distance – was his soul tie to Carmen. I'm sure she's an incredible woman with her own backstory of life's ups and downs, but as the saying goes, you can't serve two masters.

However, who knows? I'm sure there are some women who wouldn't mind their friendship, but I'm not one of those women. And I give myself full permission to know what works for me and what doesn't. Cultivating self-love is important before committing to someone, because everything doesn't work for everybody and that's ok. And when I really think about it, the truth is, I didn't have the strength to leave Randal which is why I prayed for God's help. It may have been brutal, but at least God answered my prayers.

That night I couldn't sleep. I lye awake in my hotel room listening to music until a familiar song came on: Best Part, by Daniel Caesar and HER.

It had always been me and Pierre's favorite song. I couldn't hear it and not think of him, but he had stopped speaking to me on my 39th birthday just one year before my 40th birthday. There I was one year later – alone in a hotel room – after breaking up with yet another man. Talk about going back to square one. But it was my 40th birthday and I had refused to feel like a victim. Emotionally, mentally, and spiritually, I was going to either sink or swim.

I decided to cry and allow the feelings to flow through me because I deserved to heal. And at this stage of my life, I was too smart to play tough. I was a woman. And there was nothing wrong with being sensitive. In fact, if Randal chose to leave me on my 40ᵗʰ birthday, then I chose to see it as a GIFT. I was free.

Pushing the hotel curtains to the side, I looked out the windows and sent a silent blessing out into the universe. *Thank you for answering my prayers. Thank you for bringing me to California and to this beautiful hotel room. I'm safe. I'm at peace. And I made it into my magical 40's with unlimited potential to do whatever I want!... I think I'm gonna get my "Eat, Pray, Love" on and keep traveling...*

I crawled into bed going under the sheets and lay my head on the soft pillow. It was time to rest my worries. Who cares if I was single at 40? If I disappointed my mother or any of my female friends who wanted to be part of a dream wedding, well, none of them were living my life. Only I was.

The next morning, I took my chances and called Pierre. We hadn't spoken since the BLM protests that had taken place a year before and I was hoping he wasn't still upset with me. When he answered my call, we had a heart-to-heart as I sat in the San Francisco airport, waiting to return to NY. He couldn't believe I was all the way out in California, but, when Pierre broke up with me after the George Floyd incident, I moved on months later – to coincidently end up with another African American.

Hearing his voice over the phone felt like "home." Not because I wanted him back, but because we had too much history to allow politics to be the reason we parted ways on our separate journeys.

Funny, how sometimes ex-boyfriends and ex-girlfriends can feel like comfort food when you're down. Not only do they already know you, but since you've already gone through the fire with them, there's no pretending. You've seen each other's ugly sides and so all there's left to see after you forgive each other is beauty. That's how I wanted to remember Pierre.

I guess that's why those friendships matter so much, and why Randal stayed so close to Carmen. But I still feel, even as I look back in retrospect, that your "forever person" should be your "best friend" or else, what's the point of settling down unless you settle for something less than you deserve: true happiness. And heck, when it really comes down to the nitty gritty, aren't you your own best friend anyway, which means you ultimately get to decide what's best for you – not your family and friends, or society? Gosh, I never want to rush that feeling again.

I suppose if any of us are looking for a lifetime companion, then eventually we have to choose who we want to walk into the future with, unless you're polyamorous. But if you're monogamous, then there's only room to commit to one soulmate – a choice that shouldn't be played with – not when love is supposed to be protected like a diamond, lest the world dilute its healing ability by infecting it with various voices and opinions that influence people to choose partners for all the wrong reasons other than real love.

Love is too precious to be reduced to a game of chess by moving plastic pieces across a board. We are divine beings who sometimes enjoy walking alongside another sparkling soul headed towards mutual pastures. As long as it doesn't distract you from reaching your North Star, certain lovers are there to bring out the best in you. Make room for them by saying "No" to others. As Randal's inscribed mirror message read: *Trust the Process*. What I'd like to conclude is that the purpose of the process is not to shrink your understanding of love, but to expand it. And so, developing true love feels like it should be an organic unfolding between conscious people who treat all types of relationships as divine unions – not some prized possession to grant you access into a special "Wives Club." Therefore, whether married or unmarried, we don't need to achieve marital status to measure our value, nor should we rush the development of any relationship to realize our self-worth through gaining a title.

I told Pierre that when our song, "Best Part," came on in my hotel room, that's what made me think of him. Just like the song goes, *if life were a movie, know you're the best part.* It's a shame that a game of racial tension and political upheaval had come in between our friendship a year prior to this, but through the spiritual law of forgiveness, we mended our friendship, and Pierre was there to greet me when I came back. Not as a lover, but as a former soulmate.

NYC, I was coming home – to my heart.

Chapter 9
Circling Back to My Heart-Centered Self

"How was the fire ceremony?" I asked my new friend at the glamping resort. I was turning the key to lock the door before walking over to the garden area.

She pushed her hair to the side, "Oh... you should've come. You would've loved it last night."

"I think I'll definitely try it one day, but I have to ease my way into something like that."

"You'll know when you're ready. How's you writing coming along?" She asked.

"Ahhh... this was the best place to write. You know, I have to say... getting away like this was so therapeutic. It was like a soul purge."

She smiled. "That's wonderful... I hope to read your book when it's done."

"You never know... you might be in it," I laughed. "They do say Tulum is the best place for Bachelorettes and we seem to be doing just fine on this vacation."

She giggled. "Well, before you leave, you're more than welcome to join me for dinner and drinks on your last day."

As we said our goodbyes, I went off to order my breakfast in Mexican pesos. I really did wish I could extend my vacation a little longer. Instead, I told myself I just had another reason to revisit this gorgeous paradise. The people were friendly, the prices were good, and maybe next time I wouldn't be so afraid to venture out a little more – maybe swim in one of the cenotes or party under the stars at an outdoor nightclub. If only I were this careful with my heart the way I was with other things. There's nothing wrong with being cautious. I think it's better to be safe than sorry. But it would probably do me some good to be more careful with who I gave my heart, mind, body and soul to.

After flying back into NY, I thought about all the pages I'd just written from the memories of my lived experiences, thinking about how these four men, Mike, Pierre, Kevin, and Randal had taught me different lessons.

Mike was a survivor who, although was confused about his sexual orientation, still smiled through the pain. Whistling *jingle bells* when carrying a Christmas tree through the subway station was his way of identifying with something – even if it were just to keep the holiday spirit alive. He taught me what it means to let go of someone even if you love them because their healing might be something they have to do on their own – with or without you. And during any day of the year, you can choose to forgive them and mend the past. Your love shouldn't have to be reserved for one special holiday when time itself is our most precious commodity.

Pierre taught me the importance of friendship in a relationship because he never felt obligated or guilty to be with me. Instead, he felt free to be himself. He was a music producer and Actor struggling to make ends meet, but regardless of how low funds were, we always enjoyed the time of our lives. We never needed money for fancy dates. All we needed was each other because we were loved for who we were, not for what we had – and that made our connection priceless. Especially, when we recorded a Nina Simone remake of "West Wind", renaming it "North Star", creating a body of work that was born from the love of music we both shared.

Kevin showed me not to judge a book by its cover. An army soldier-turned NJ Sheriff who loved the easy life by jamming reggae music in beachy towns, may have given the impression of a "tough guy" because of his police uniform, but he actually didn't even like violence. It was just an easy transition from his military background, and if he could've had it his way, he would've patrolled a quiet beach all day taking in the sun. However, maybe the fact that he didn't get to apply for that job location back when he was married, is was made him decide never to compromise his happiness again. A lifestyle choice or preference has the power to affect the trajectory of a lot of other important things too.

And so, despite our last "date night" having been at the Madison Square Garden basketball game, I learned that life is not a game to be played with when your intuition compels you to do something – or not to do something. Pre-pandemic, he felt something in his gut telling him to stay away from the city, and that was before the George Floyd protests broke out across all major cities just three months later. In hindsight, I realize that timing is everything. And sometimes world events occur that take precedence over our plans because there's a greater force at play. Hence, love is not only meant for some people; it's meant for *everyone* – just another reason to trust your intuition when a higher guidance speaks through it. I'm glad Kevin listened to his intuition, which must've brought him to a lifestyle more aligned with his desires – hopefully, somewhere near a beach.

Lastly, Randal taught me about the power of taking chances even before you're ready. Neither of us were looking for love when we were introduced, but we jumped on the opportunity to meet despite being in the midst of a worldwide pandemic. Almost immediately after my grandmother's burial from Covid, I was flown across country during a time when most people remained quarantined at home. The only thing I did push away, however, was a possible marriage proposal because we were in the process of manifesting it when ring shopping. Aside from that, not every relationship is meant to last forever but that doesn't mean we should devalue the blessing it was when you were together.

Randal invited me into a world of nature, showing me how meditation comes in many forms including walking through the woods. There's an element of focus when the only sound you hear are little branches breaking from squirrels running through Forest trees, or birds chirping after leaping from their nests to fly through the wind. It was Randal's leadership skills of bringing me out West that showed me what's possible for my life if I change environments. Maybe I didn't like the idea of him keeping an ex-girlfriend around who was still in love with him, but that didn't mean I didn't appreciate all the other gifts he shared: generosity, communication, and the intention to pursue a spiritually conscious path.

And with that, I also learned that while certain roads are good for our growth, others might be a little too risky. Taking chances involves a bit of fearlessness within the confinements of certain limitations. Once you step outside the lines of self-love, that's when walking towards the edge becomes a little too far, and you have to come back to center: yourself.

Once I jiggled my keys through my apartment door, I was greeted by my two slender grey cats, Pantha and Jay. I hadn't mentioned them until now because the story highlighted romantic love, however, the bond I shared with these furry little angels is something no boyfriend or husband could ever understand. You know how they say a dog is a man's best friend? Well, I offer the possibility that a cat is a woman's. As I took turns lifting each cat into my arms to squeeze them tightly, I felt I had everything I ever needed: companionship, freedom, and unconditional love. Not to mention, how often those cats used to hear me sing through the rooms!

The truth is those cats witnessed my growth in stages, accompanying my younger years as a soulful house singer writing music off my laptop, to cuddling beside me every night when I transitioned into the nine to five world and started crawling into bed early. Through the years, layers of myself would fall off for other parts to emerge. It's part of the reason I struggled at one-point in time, thinking I needed to change who I was in order to settle down. Now I know that whether you settle down with one person or end up experiencing many, love is all around. It's found in friendships, both old and new; it's found in family whether near or far, and most importantly, it's found in you because you are the center in which every other relationship stems from. As a newfound Yoga Teacher, I learned that the partners we attract are determined by how brightly our aura shines from a well-balanced full body chakra alignment with the heart chakra being one of the most important.

After settling back into my apartment, my cousin Linda and I connected on social media to make sure we both made it home safely, followed by updating our Tulum profile pictures.

The two of us, back home feeling safe, rested, and soulfully recharged by Mexico's magical healing, flooded our newsfeeds with tropical pictures of a well-deserved and much needed vacation. I confidently predict more exciting journeys are on the horizon.

Attention all bachelorette's, I affirm Tulum is the place to be – not only for beach partying, but also for the chance to walk along the pearly white sand and connect with Mother Earth's universal language: Amor.

It is so much more than romance; so much more than politics; so much more than status; so much more than money; and so much more than skin color. Love is spiritual. And it starts with you.

ABOUT THE AUTHOR

AUTHOR: Jasmine Clemente

Born and raised in NYC, Jasmine Clemente, began her creative career as a Soulful House Singer before moonlighting into other artistic avenues such as storytelling, blogging, and recording audio meditations. Through intuitive guidance, she connects personal trauma to self-healing by mindfully writing and speaking in a way that teaches audiences how to find the "divine message's" in life's "beautiful mess." She's also an international Yoga Teacher, sharing her favorite spiritual practices that kept her grounded amid the ebbs and flows of human existence.

JASMINE CLEMENTE
publishing

ABOUT THE
COVER DESIGNER

BOOK COVER DESIGNER: Margo Bobrowicz

Inspired by European Renaissance art, Margo Bobrowicz, is a talented Graphic Artist based in the UK who creates elegant images for book covers, Tarot cards, portraits, and more. Discovered on the World Wide Web, this Poland raised beauty captures the essence of each subject's true spirit by highlighting their best traits, all while revealing the magical thread that interweaves the timeless connection of human evolution, whether ancient, modern or otherwise.

ABOUT THE PUBLISHING PARTNER

BOOK COACH: Hammad

Hammad is a dedicated publishing professional and founder of Hmdpublishing. With years of experience in book formatting, cover design, and the publishing process, Hammad has helped countless authors bring their stories to life. Specialising in Kindle Direct Publishing (KDP) and other major platforms, he ensures every book is presented with the highest quality standards, whether for print or eBook formats. Passionate about storytelling and design, Hammad takes pride in collaborating with authors to create works that truly resonate with readers.